MERRY & SEDUCED

SHELLEY MUNRO

MUNRO PRESS

Merry & Seduced

Copyright © 2024 by Shelley Munro

Print ISBN: 978-1-99-106374-8
Ebook ISBN: 978-0-473-30358-7

Editor: Mary Moran
Cover: Kim Killion, The Killion Group, Inc.

Munro Press, New Zealand.

First Munro Press electronic publication November 2014
First Munro Press print publication December 2024

DEDICATION

For Paul, my husband, partner in crime, and fellow adventurer.
Every day is a good day.

INTRODUCTION

All roads lead home at Christmas...

Cyborg Amme Vanak is wired to care for children and since her current charge is grown, she's feeling edgy. She's hoping a Christmas visit to Earth with her friends will offer distraction and maybe even a fling with a sexy Earthman before she flies on to Viros for a new adventure.

Wealthy entrepreneur Marcus Polo is single with a rockin' social life until an unexpected Christmas gift throws his existence into chaos. A chance meeting with exotic Amme deepens his turmoil. She might be the solution to his problem, but she's different from his exes, and she pushes every one of his sexual buttons.

Amme is torn. Marcus Polo is handsome and kind and so, so

attractive. Even better, it seems the fascination is mutual. Amme is having a ball on Earth, but as departure day creeps closer, she becomes increasingly conflicted about leaving. Then there's the whole alien thing. Somehow, she doesn't think Earth and Marcus are ready to accept aliens are fact and not science fiction.

Warning: Contains a bunch of aliens intent on relaxing and enjoying a New Zealand Christmas, some canoodling under the mistletoe and addictions to chocolate.

CHAPTER ONE

A snippet of a Christmas carol blasted through Marcus Polo's concentration, and he clicked on an icon to bring up the inter-office memo. He read the note from his long-time secretary and frowned.

He wrote, *Sign for the package*, and hit send.

Seconds later, the lyrics about snow and deer announced another memo.

He insists you personally sign for the package.

Marcus rolled back his chair and stood. Impatience simmered through him as he stalked for his office door and yanked it open. "Cynthia, why can't you sign for the package? What's so important—"

"You the Polo dude?" A rail-thin courier smacked a wad of gum and shifted it to bulge in his cheek. "Marcus Polo?"

"Yes." Marcus stared at the kid, who couldn't be much older

than twenty. His long blond hair was restrained in a complicated plait, and he wore several rings in one ear. The other ear lobe stretched around a black disc.

"Is your middle name Craig?"

Marcus's brows shot up. "Pardon?"

"I've already confirmed the details for him, but he insisted on speaking directly to you." Red-cheeked but with not a blonde hair out of place, Cynthia stood by the corner of her desk, her right stiletto tapping her irritation.

"Is your name Marcus Craig Polo?" The kid shuffled the gum to his other cheek.

"Yes."

The kid nodded. "Good. Sign here for your package."

"What package?" Marcus asked.

"It's out in the hall. There's this letter to go with it." He shoved an electronic pad at Marcus. "Sign here."

Marcus signed using the stylus and the kid handed him the letter.

"I'll get the package for you." He disappeared into the hall and returned a few seconds later carrying a small suitcase and leading a child by the hand. "This is your package. Have a good day."

The child—a girl—took one look at Marcus and started howling. Tears poured down her cheeks, and Marcus shot Cynthia a helpless look, his mind reeling. Shock, confusion, helplessness. The emotions took the opportunity to kick him in the gut before moving on to leave panic jabbing his temples.

"Perhaps I should reschedule your appointments." Cynthia darted around her desk and dropped onto her chair, hurriedly distancing herself from Marcus's package. The rapid tap of her fingers on her keyboard a full stop on her *don't-pick-me* attitude. Obviously, some things she considered outside her secretarial duties.

Marcus studied the child. "What's your name, sweetheart?"

His renowned charm failed him this time. Epic fail since the howls increased, interspersed with noisy sniffles.

Cynthia winced, and Marcus decided to retreat. He scooped up the child and held her much like a rugby ball as he sped into his office. He set her down, shut his door with a firm click and opened the envelope.

Dear Marcus,

I know this will come as a huge shock to you, but meet your daughter, Autumn Lana Polo. You are her last living relative since if you're receiving this letter, I'm already dead from ovarian cancer.

She really is your daughter—a DNA test will prove that soon enough—and I hope you will keep her and look after her until she is old enough to become independent. The Polo family has a long pedigree, and while your family isn't particularly close, our daughter should know her history and her relations. She'll need those roots to grow and flourish.

Autumn is a good kid, although right now, she's probably terrified. She has a loud wail on her. I think she gets that from me since I'm sure you haven't changed over the years and still keep your emotional distance when it comes to relationships. I bet you still possess your trademark playboy gene. You'll have to change now that you have responsibility for our daughter, and that's not a bad thing, no matter what your thoughts as you read this.

Autumn doesn't have any allergies. She's had some of the normal childhood illnesses, which are included on the attached list, along with her birth certificate and passport.

If I'd known about the cancer, I'd have done things differently and

5

approached you earlier. Please look upon our daughter as a precious gift rather than a burden and do the right thing. I beg of you this one thing. Despite our differences, I know you're an honorable man.

Keep our daughter safe.
Candice Kane

Marcus read the letter again, but the contents didn't change. He raised a shaky hand to his forehead and wiped the moisture away. He blinked. The wording didn't disappear. The child—Autumn—continued crying. Nope, denial wasn't working.

He had a daughter.

A problem because he didn't have a single bloody idea of what to do with one.

It wasn't as if he'd thought about kids. They were something for the future.

He had a daughter.

Hell's bells.

At least the crying had decreased in decibels. He studied her red, blotchy face. It was wet with tears, and...dear God...that was snot.

Tissues.

He needed tissues.

Pleased to come to some sort of a decision, even if it was an attempt to stem the tears, he strode to his computer and typed a memo to Cynthia.

A light tap sounded on his door. It cracked open and a hand holding a bright red box appeared in the gap.

"Come in, Cynthia," Marcus said.

Cynthia did but every muscle of her curvy body shouted reluctance. "I'm a secretary, not a nanny. Just in case you're getting ideas."

Marcus scowled. "Message received. Have you rearranged my

schedule?"

"Yes."

"Good. I'll be out for the rest of the day. I'll let you know later if I need the rest of the week shifted around."

"Very well. I'll continue with the Fargo Freight and Shipping acquisition," Cynthia said.

"Call me if you need anything," Marcus said. "It appears I'll be working from home in the near future." His cell phone beeped, signaling an incoming message, and Cynthia paused in case he needed her to undertake another task.

Ring me. Sophie, xxx.

"Not happening." He cursed under his breath and deleted the text. Bloody Sophie Robinson didn't appear to understand the word, no. "If Sophie Robinson happens to ring for me again, tell her I'm not in and I will never be in when she calls."

"Ouch. Will do, boss man. Told you that woman was a clingy mistake. And this is another." With a jerk of her head toward the child, Cynthia disappeared, closing the door behind her with a sharp click that said she wanted nothing to do with this business. Marcus couldn't blame her. This tiny girl child made him want to flee too.

He pulled several tissues from the box and crouched beside his daughter. Funny, but he didn't doubt the truth of Candice's letter. They'd had an affair—a brief but passionate liaison that had ended almost before it started. He'd made it clear he wasn't interested in a permanent relationship, just as he'd stated the sentiment to the women who came after Candice.

Condoms—he used them religiously. He'd never had sex without a condom, but in this case, the birth control method had failed.

Autumn had the same shade of hair as him—a burnished chestnut brown—that made her name fit perfectly. Her eyes were the same shade of brown he saw in the mirror each day. Yes, even without the DNA test, he was certain Autumn was his child.

But what to do with her?

That was the problem.

He sucked in a deep breath and stared at Autumn. She stared back, seeming to appraise him in the same way he was measuring her. "Why don't we wipe away some of those tears and blow your nose?"

"'Kay," she whispered.

Encouraged by her response, he blotted up her tears and grabbed another handful of tissues.

"I can do it," she said, her small hands fighting his for control of the paper hankies.

"All right," he said and rocked back on his heels.

She had his determination too, and this spurt of character decided him. He couldn't foist her off on his parents—not that they'd entertain the idea. Besides, he refused to subject any child to their chilly methods of rearing offspring. The idea of handing her off to Child Services made him a little queasy, which left one alternative.

He'd keep her.

But that didn't solve his immediate problem. Kids were a big mystery to him. He shot her another quick glance and saw she was managing well. Hell, he didn't even know her age.

"How old are you?"

"Three and three-quarters," she said.

Okay. That was definitive.

None of his friends had kids except...

Ah, the sweet scent of relief. He felt his lips curl into a broad smile. The knowledge of a solution within his grasp soothed the rough edges of his panic, allowed him to breathe.

Max and Ellen O'Sullivan had one boy and another kid on the way. Perfect.

"All done?"

She nodded, and her bottom lip trembled again. She started to squirm, stepping from one foot to the other. "I need the toilet."

Marcus cursed under his breath and cursed again—long and loud—in the privacy of his mind. He figured he'd be doing that a lot in the future. He grasped her little hand, awed by the perfection of her tiny fingers and the bright pink nail polish. With his other hand, he grabbed his car keys off his desk and patted his jacket to make sure he had his wallet. He paused to stuff his phone in his pocket.

"Let's go," he said. "Once we've got you sorted out, we'll go for a ride in the car."

"I'm hungry," she said, her glance uncertain.

"I think we can handle that," he said, and she rewarded him with a shy smile. A sharp tug in the region of his heart froze him in position for long seconds, and he fell a little bit in love with his new daughter at that moment.

Yep, no doubt about it—no matter the problems, the inconvenience.

He was keeping her.

"Do my ears look pointy in this?" Kaya asked, cocking her head so her blue hair swung away to reveal a jeweled ear cuff.

"Very funny." Camryn O'Sullivan plucked at her hair in telltale irritation. "Tell them, Ry. None of them are taking this seriously. Earth isn't ready for aliens. It's gonna be bad enough facing my brother and his wife again after all these months. I don't want to worry about the population of New Zealand panicking because they think it's an alien invasion."

Amme Vanak stood in the background, leaning against a wall of the flight deck of the *Indefatigable*, a smirk tugging her lips.

This argument had been ongoing ever since Ry announced they'd visit Earth for Christmas. A summer Christmas since they were going to the southern hemisphere, and she couldn't wait. The conversation never failed to entertain her, and she suspected the crew enjoyed teasing Camryn.

"What do you say, Amme?" Nanu, the ship's engineer and pilot, drew her into the discussion. The beads on the ends of his braids clacked as his attention shifted from her back to Camryn. "Do you want to do some sightseeing on Earth?"

Of course she did. "As long as I can regulate my skin tone."

Her cyborg nature allowed her to change her skin tone to blend. Her other characteristics were less noticeable. When she was a child, the categorization committee on her home planet of Sheng had determined she would profit their society most by entering the profession of childcare. Then, like all children on Sheng, she'd undergone enhancements to complement her natural inclinations.

Her enhancements included increased empathy for children, the ability to think and learn quickly, extra physical strength and stamina to keep up with the young and fend off attacks on her charges if necessary. Perfect eyesight. Excellent hearing. Perfect health and antibodies added to guard against most known diseases. On Earth, she'd appear humanoid. She was luckier in that respect than Kaya, with her pointed ears and bright blue hair, or Gweneth, with the cat tattoo on her cheek, and Mogens, who flashed from black to white depending on his mood.

"I have the solution for those of us who don't appear humanoid." Mogens violet eyes sparkled in his white face—an indication of happiness and contentment. "Never fear. We shall all visit Camryn's family. We shall have fun. I have read this in the clouds."

A spurt of excitement fizzled through Amme, and she grinned at Mogens. Camryn had told them so much about Earth, and they were eager to explore and experience a New Zealand Christmas.

The southern hemisphere. Hot weather. Beaches. Barbecues.

"What sort of solution? Have you trialed it?" Camryn asked, suspicion coloring her tone while her gaze sliced and diced, forging a path to the truth.

"On myself." Mogens' long broad nose lifted in a show of dignity. "My appearance represents the biggest challenge since it fluctuates from black to white and in between. The cream I've developed turns my skin a golden brown. If I change my robes for those things you called jeans and a T-shirt, I'll pass as a human." He winked at Amme.

Amme felt her mouth drop open. Well! Mogens was very pleased with himself.

"Fine, that's one problem solved, but where are you going to hide the Indefatigable?" Camryn asked, spearing each of them with a glower in turn. "You can't just park it in the middle of a paddock and leave it there. My brother is going to notice. His employees and neighbors are sure to remark on a hulking big spaceship parked on the lawn."

"Nanu and I have a plan," Mogens said.

"Of course you do," Camryn said drily.

Ry placed his hands on Camryn's shoulders and pulled her against his chest. His handsome features held a wealth of tenderness as he stroked his mate's shoulder and arm. "Stop worrying. We have the *Indy* covered. No one will come upon our ship. I've told you this. Your brother will be pleased to see you."

"I hope so."

Amme moved forward to stand beside the woman who'd become a close friend. They'd spent a lot of the voyage together, discussing their lives and sharing personal experiences. "Of course he will. Once he gets over his shock, I'm sure he'll be excited to see you. Are you going to tell him about becoming a feline shifter? That you're no longer fully human like him because you mated with Ry?"

"Maybe." Camryn's brow creased then she pulled away from Ry to pace back and forth in front of the view screen. Her boots beat a tattoo on the bridge floor, the sound becoming increasingly rapid as her mind wrestled with her fear. "I guess. He's not going to believe a human can turn into a black leopard without a demonstration."

Amme exchanged a glance with Ry.

"Let's go and workout," Ry said. "It will rid you of some of your nerves."

"If workout is code for sex, then I'm staying here to help Nanu," Jannike, Ry's second-in-command said. Built like an assassin warrior, the tall blonde woman maintained a serious mien. Most thought she lacked humor. Amme knew better. The woman hid her humor bone and soft heart. She often acted the champion for those who were weaker and unable to stand up for themselves.

Camryn's troubled gaze swept them, and she let out a huge sigh. "This visit is going to be a disaster. I just know it."

"Is the shield on? No one can see us land, right? The military forces won't shoot us out of the sky?" Camryn's voice dripped with anxiety, and Amme noted her friend's fingers curl and uncurl, twist and untwist at her sides.

A ship of the frigate category, the *Indy* was a huge hulk and built to undertake long space voyages. Its somber gray color wasn't flashy like some of the cruise ships, and that would help it blend during their approach, but Amme understood Camryn's anxiety. From the moment they'd entered Earth's atmosphere, they courted danger.

"Shields are fully functional," Ry said in a clipped tone that indicated this landing was more difficult than any of them admitted. "The *Indy* is invisible to tracking devices and the naked eye."

Jannike planted her hands on her hips and scowled her tough-warrior glare. "Camryn, if you don't shut up, Kaya and I are gonna gag you. I don't care what Ry says. If the Earth military had noticed our entry into the atmosphere, they would have sent fighter ships to intercept us by now." She crossed to her seat next to Nanu and clipped the safety harness into place.

Amme grabbed Camryn by the arm and dragged her over to one of the rear seats. They both buckled their harnesses while the others studied the instrument panel, and Nanu manipulated the controls. "Tell me about the men on Earth. Do you think I'll manage to find one for a Christmas fling?"

Camryn ripped her gaze off the clouds beyond the view port and turned to her with raised brows. "You want a man?"

"I didn't say I wanted to keep him," Amme said. "*Ooh*, pretty. Look at the trees. Is that a river?"

"Amme, you can't drop a man bomb without telling me more."

Ah, her distraction had worked. She turned from the view to focus on Camryn. "Now that Gweneth has blossomed and become independent, she doesn't need me. I was designed to look after others, and the lack of need in that department is making me...unsettled." Yes, that was the correct word to describe her current unease.

"But an affair? Really?" Camryn said, diverted from her anxiety as Amme had intended.

"Memories to keep me warm on the long space voyage to Viros."

The engine roared extra loud, there was a metallic bang, and the Indy tilted at a forty-degree angle without warning, flinging Amme against her harness. Over at the control panel, Nanu cursed. An alarm burst into life.

Jannike echoed him with equally pithy sentiments. "Grata, watch out! We're gonna crash."

"Don't you think I know that," Nanu said, his tone testy.

"Sit-rep," Ry demanded.

Nanu checked the panels, his instruments, stabbed at buttons. "One of the stabilizers isn't working. Don't know why."

"Hard right," Ry ordered. "Right or we'll hit those trees."

"I said I know that," Nanu snapped.

Ry shot a glower at his mate. "Camryn, the clearing you mentioned isn't where you said it would be."

"Sorry." Camryn winced. "I wasn't at my best the last time I was here. I did tell you that."

"I see the clearing," Nanu said, his shoulders straining and fighting the thruster control. "Turn, damn it. Turn!"

"Can you straighten our approach?" Ry asked, his voice calm.

Nanu's beefy hands raced over the control panel while his gaze remained on the rapidly approaching landscape. "It's a thruster. A malfunction. It's fukked up the landing stabilizers and the steering. Turn, Indy."

Amme gripped her seat handrests and stared out the view screen at the landscape. Despite Nanu's attempts, the *Indy* was still flying at a drunken angle. The trees appeared enormous this close. She swallowed. "That's assuming we make it to the ground in one piece. I might be all talk about this fling if we crash and die."

The engine roared, and Nanu fought the controls. Slowly, the *Indy* started to level.

Beside them, Kaya snorted out a laugh. "Don't worry. We'll land safely. I want one of those sex flings too. I'm counting on it. We haven't hit many planets where the males have the right working parts. Need to make sure I haven't gone rusty."

"Your brother would hatch an Earth animal...an elephant if he heard you say that, Kaya," Jannike said.

"What he don't know won't hurt him," Kaya said with a cheeky wink over her shoulder. "Earth fling, here I come."

Camryn barked out a laugh and shot an impish glance at Ry.

"Maybe I should try a fling. They sound like fun."

"Not if you know what's good for you," Ry said. "Ease it down, Nanu. We're almost at the clearing."

"She's not responding. Darlin', I need you level. Damn it. Jannike, you'll have to manipulate the manual landing gear," Nanu said, his attention on the controls. "Hurry."

"I can't reach," Jannike snapped. "Hang on." She unclicked her safety harness just as the frigate slanted in the other direction. Her feet went from under her and she slid across the floor, landing against a panel of instruments, headfirst. "*Oomph.*"

"You're in the right place now," Nanu said urgently. "Pull the red lever."

Jannike groaned, and Amme saw a trickle of blood rolling down the second officer's cheek. Her movements were sluggish, and she missed her grab for the handhold when the Indy rolled again. She shot across the floor and thudded into another control panel just as the Indy struck the ground. "Grata, Nanu. Can't you fly this thing straight?"

"Doing my best. Get the lever," Nanu ordered.

"Fukk you," Jannike said and swiped some of the blood off her cheek. She half scuttled, half crawled across the floor toward the lever. She reached out, grabbed hold. "Got it."

The *Indy* bounced. Amme's stomach dropped, and she jolted against her safety harness, her gaze on Jannike instead of the landscape and the green of trees whizzing past the view port. The *Indy* punched into the terrain. Jumped. Hit.

Jannike moaned with each successive smack. Amme's harness dug into her shoulders. She grunted. Beside her, Camryn growled, her feline rattled by the rough ride.

"Hang tight. We're gonna hit again," Nanu warned.

Outside, tree branches gouged the hull with nasty metallic shrieks. Amme's receptors prickled at the sharp scratches, the small hairs at the back of her neck rising.

"Come on, sweetheart," Nanu crooned from between tight lips. The engines roared as the *Indy* battled gravity.

Jannike tried to right herself, to scuttle across the floor, but the Indy bucked and shrieked like a defiant *beest*. She cursed. Tensed to avoid another body slam as she slid, unable to gain purchase. "Can you please help instead of showing off?"

"One more hop should do it," Nanu said. "They're getting smaller."

The Indy struck, and the entire frigate groaned as if the landing pained her, too.

Amme waited for the ship to lift again. When it remained in place, she unclipped her safety harness and hurried over to Jannike. "Where does it hurt?"

"My head," Jannike said with a glare at Nanu. "It was his bad driving."

"You took off your safety harness," Ry said. "Last time you did that you hit your noggin too."

"And both times I was trying to help," Jannike said. "You're the captain. You should have volunteered."

"Do I look stupid?" Ry smirked at her, and Amme had difficulty holding back a laugh. The crew constantly sniped at each other, yet if anyone dared attack, they fought the foe as one strong unit.

"Do you think anyone noticed us landing?" Camryn asked.

"We've left a trail of destruction," Kaya said. "We hit trees."

"This visit is doomed," Camryn said. "*Doomed*. This is a sign. We should leave right now."

"Coward," Ry said.

Camryn's back straightened, and another catlike growl emerged from deep in her throat.

"Stop teasing your mate. Watch my finger," Amme said to Jannike, and she waggled it from left to right in front of the second-in-command's face. Jannike followed orders, and Amme nodded in satisfaction. "Normal reaction. She has a bump on her skull, but she'll live. I'll clean up the blood for you."

Mogens hurried onto the flight deck. "If it's safe to leave the ship, I'll plant a spell, one to repel anyone who comes too close. You're positive the atmosphere is safe?"

"It's safe," Camryn said. "But take a reading first. It's a good habit."

Nanu's fingers danced over the controls. "I'll put the shield in place. There. Done. Anyone looking at the *Indy* will see what he or she expects to see. Trees and more trees."

"But what about the gouges in the earth and the broken trees?" Camryn demanded. "And the sound of our arrival."

A trace of black swirled into Mogens pale skin, giving him streaks of gray on his chin and jaw. "My spell will work with the damage," he said, his tone offended. "Hopefully, the black clouds on the horizon will get the blame for the noise."

"Is it gonna rain?" Jannike climbed to her feet with a tortured groan. "That's all we need. It rained last time we came to this planet. Ry stunk out the tender with his wet fur."

"No," Mogens said. "The clouds are traveling away from our direction. The sunshine will remain."

"Well, that's something," Jannike grumbled.

"Take a seat," Amme said, but her attention wandered to Camryn before she opened the med-box and selected an absorbent pad. "I'll doctor your ouchies." Now that they'd arrived, Camryn couldn't keep still. She paced the flight deck and did several circuits until Ry grasped her hand and hauled her against his side. Even so, she vibrated with her trepidation. This reunion with her family scared her, and it showed.

"We're going right now," Ry said. "We'll leave Nanu and the others in charge of the ship, and we'll go and tell your brother we're here."

Camryn looked as if she might throw up. "No, we'll go tomorrow. I—"

"Camryn, you need to go now, or you'll make yourself sick with worry," Amme said.

"You come with us," Camryn said and turned a beseeching expression on her. "Please."

Amme exchanged a glance with Ry and he nodded.

"All right. Let me finish treating Jannike, then I'll adjust my skin color, and I'm ready to go," Amme said and peered at Jannike's forehead. "The bleeding has almost stopped." She sprayed it with an anti-stop to halt the last of the bleeding, observed for a sec and nodded in approval. "A medi-pad, and you'll be done."

"What about us?" Kaya asked.

"I'll take you to meet my brother and sister-in-law tomorrow. All of you," Camryn said. "I promise."

Amme glanced at Camryn's skin color and willed her own natural bronze tones to lighten. It took mere seconds. Yes, that was better. She'd blend now.

"I've got my com if you run in to any problems. Don't hesitate to contact me," Ry said.

"Likewise," Jannike said. "We can be there quickly if you strike trouble."

"We're visiting Camryn's family on a peaceful planet. There won't be any trouble."

CHAPTER TWO

Amme thought Camryn might faint as she stood before the front door of a rambling white bungalow. All her natural sparkle had fled to leave extreme pallor, and she looked as if she were having trouble breathing, as if someone had kicked her in the gut and knocked the air from her lungs. Her breaths seesawed in and out, an audible statement of fear.

Amme exchanged a glance with Ry, saw his concern, the way his jaw firmed and almost felt sorry for the people on the other side of the door.

"I'll knock on the door," Amme said and rapped her knuckles against the wood. "Your family will be pleased to see you."

"Someone is coming." Ry sniffed to ascertain the degree of danger and relaxed. "The scent holds a touch of you. It's one of your family."

Camryn swallowed audibly, her gaze fixed on the doorway.

Amme suspected her friend wanted to run, but Ry's arm around her waist and her unsteady legs rooted her to the spot.

The door opened to a child. Luke. He was four, Amme remembered from Camryn's stories. He loved horses and other animals, taking after his father and Camryn in that respect.

"Luke," Camryn croaked.

The boy looked at her and burst into a wide grin. "Auntie Cam. Auntie Cam. Auntie Cam!"

"He remembers me," Camryn croaked again.

"Of course he does," Amme said.

"Auntie Cam!" Luke shrieked.

A woman appeared in the passage behind them, her belly swollen with child in the Earth way. This must be Ellen, Amme decided and smiled in welcome. She was tiny with blonde hair and bright blue eyes, just as Camryn had described.

Ellen glanced at Amme and Ry and waddled to the door, a polite expression of inquiry settling on her neat features. Then she spotted Camryn, and her mouth twisted into anger. Disdain. This woman had judged her friend and found her lacking.

"What are you doing here? Max spent weeks looking for you. Weeks of checking bars and the hospital. We filed a missing person's report."

"I-I'm sorry," Camryn said. "I-I—"

"You can't just turn up and expect a welcome," Ellen spat. "I want you to leave before Max comes. You've caused enough trouble, and we—I can't take anymore. You're irresponsible, Camryn, and a drunk. Just go." She shoved Camryn hard, pushing her back two steps. "We don't want you here."

"That's enough," Ry said, and he thrust Camryn behind him and out of Ellen's reach.

"Who are you?" Ellen demanded.

"I am Camryn's mate."

Amme realized the woman didn't have a translator. Ry's words would sound like unintelligent garble.

"This is Ryman Coppersmith, my mate. This is Amme Vanak, our friend," Camryn said, apparently understanding the problem. She'd taught them English, but Ry had forgotten to use his learning in the heat of the moment.

"I don't care," Ellen said. "Just go before Max gets back."

A vehicle pulled into the driveway, and Ellen's lips pressed together. A flash of temper colored her cheeks with pink before she gave a hard sigh of resignation.

Amme turned to inspect the new arrival. Camryn gasped, took half a step, and halted in indecision.

The vehicle screeched to a stop, and the driver's door flung open. "Camryn?" a hoarse voice demanded.

The new arrival was a masculine version of Camryn. He raked a hand through his hair, shaggy and in need of a cut, and tugged off his sunglasses. He was a fraction taller, but it was obvious they were siblings.

"Max," Camryn murmured, then they both were running.

Max's arms tightened around her and he buried his face against her shoulder. After a long hug, they pulled back to stare at each other.

"Where have you been?" Max asked, his voice hoarse and throbbing with emotion. He blinked rapidly, as if to dispel a mirage, and reached out to seize Camryn's hand. His fingers wove with hers, and he clasped tight. "I searched for you everywhere. You vanished, and no one had seen you. Where the hell have you been?"

Camryn swallowed, shot a panicked glance at Ry, then glanced at Amme in a silent plea for help.

Ry and Amme had discussed this earlier, out of Camryn's earshot, and both remained silent. Camryn needed to do this on her own.

"Camryn?" Max's voice was stern, forceful, demanding answers.

"I was kidnapped by aliens," Camryn blurted.

Amme saw the scorn form in Ellen, the disappointment on Max's features, and realized Camryn had been right to worry.

"Surely you could do better than that?" Ellen asked.

Max pulled away from Camryn and stalked over to his wife.

"I told you to leave," Ellen said. "We don't need you in our lives."

A tear rolled down Camryn's cheek. Her throat worked but she didn't say anything, didn't refute their words, didn't defend herself from their verbal attack.

"Haven't you got anything to say, Camryn?" Max asked. "The truth, perhaps?"

Camryn gaped at her twin. Another tear spilled free.

"Let's go inside, Max. You can't let Camryn drag us down. She'll destroy us too." Ellen urged her husband into the house and shooed their son before them.

"Wait," Amme said, almost at the same time as Ry issued a catlike yowl.

Max and Ellen froze. Max turned, a blend of shock and indecisiveness darting through his expression before settling into resignation.

"Please, just listen to me," Camryn said. "Let us come inside so I can tell you where I've been, and if you still want me to go after I've told you my story, I'll leave without an argument."

"Max," Ellen said in warning.

Max glanced at his wife then back at his sister. "Ten minutes," he said finally and steered his wife into the house.

Camryn hesitated, squared her shoulders and strode after her brother.

Amme and Ry grinned at each other as they fell into step. Camryn was back.

Inside a room furnished with comfortable chairs, pictures of landscapes, and family photos, they found Max and Ellen seated together. Camryn fidgeted as if she needed to pace but wanted to appear calm in front of her brother and sister-in-law.

Ry headed straight for his mate, and Amme took possession of a lone chair. She settled into the plush brown cushioning and willed Camryn to do this right. Amme knew how much this meant to her friend.

Camryn loved her twin very much and hated knowing she'd disappointed him, loathed the way she'd fallen apart after the death of Gabriel, her first husband.

"We're waiting," Ellen prompted, her tone a hairsbreadth from sarcasm.

Camryn gave a jerky nod. She swallowed and started from the beginning, just as she had when she'd told the story to Amme.

"I'd been drinking," Camryn said, her chin lifting at Ellen's snort. "I'd come into the house to see you, Max. I overheard you and Ellen talking. Ellen told you I'd fallen asleep while babysitting Luke. She wasn't happy with me, and I don't blame her. The day before you'd told me I needed help and I'd rejected your suggestion to check myself into a clinic. I left the house without talking to you and went to my cottage. When my brain wouldn't let me sleep, I grabbed your old coat and went outside for a walk. That's when the aliens grabbed me."

"Really?" Ellen burst out in disbelief. "You're sticking with that story?"

Easy to see Max's disbelief. Amme and Ry had discussed this too. Amme stood and went to flank Camryn. Ry gave her a quick nod, and Amme let her skin change to its normal bronze. Ry flung off his shirt and rapidly shifted to feline.

Ellen gasped and held her belly in a protective manner. Max cursed softly before sending his wife an apologetic grin.

"The aliens," Camryn continued, "actually wanted you, Max. They wanted a horse trainer, and they grabbed me instead. They'd obtained photos of you in your coat and didn't discover they had the wrong person until they'd left to meet the Indy—their ship."

"Auntie Cam," Luke said. "Pat the kitty."

"Luke, come and sit by Mummy," Ellen ordered.

Luke cast a look of longing at Ry, ambled two steps closer.

"Luke," Max said.

Camryn's nephew ran to the two-seater and squeezed between his parents.

"I talked them into keeping me and offered to train their hell-horse. Max, it was the craziest experience I've ever had. Hell-horses are different from our horses. They promised to return me home once the race was over."

"So you're home for good?" Max asked. "You're looking much better."

"No, Max. I fell in love with Ry." Her hand landed on Ry's silky head, and he leaned into her, giving a contented purr.

So sweet, Amme thought and wondered how it would feel to have a man like Ry in her life.

"Ry is my mate. We're here for the holidays, then we're leaving to travel to Viros, Ry's birthplace," Camryn said.

"This is a nightmare," Ellen muttered. "It's not real."

Ry growled, long and low.

"Maybe we should give them the universal translators," Amme said. "That way they can understand all of us."

Camryn nodded. "Our ship's healer gave me some translator patches. Can I give you all one? They won't harm you, but it would make it easier if you could understand all of us."

"All?" Max asked. "How many of you are there?"

"Five more crew back at the ship," Camryn said.

"Five," Ellen said, her voice faint. "I don't believe this."

"Max, would you like a translator?" Camryn asked.

"Yes." Her brother stood and approached Camryn. "What do I do?"

"Press this patch behind your ear. Mogens has designed it to work for several months, and it's waterproof."

"Max, I don't know—" Ellen began.

"You raced an alien horse?" Max asked. "Did you win? God, it's so good to see you. I was worried sick. I've spent every spare moment searching for you." His voice cracked, and he cleared his throat before speaking again. "Never thought of a spaceship."

"I'm sorry. I didn't have any way of contacting you," Camryn said.

"Kitty," Luke cried, and before Ellen could stop him, he darted past his father and leaped on Ry.

Camryn laughed, and Amme chuckled at the surprise on Ry's feline face.

"Ride! Ride!" Luke shouted gleefully and dug his heels into Ry's side.

"You heard my nephew," Camryn said. "Give him a ride then shift back and say hello to my brother."

Ry grunted but did as Camryn instructed. He navigated the furniture with the child clinging to his back and chortling gleefully.

"Go, horsey. Go," Luke shouted, using his hands and heels in the manner of a jockey.

Camryn affixed the translator patch for her brother.

"Do you understand me?" Amme asked, speaking her native language from Sheng.

"Yes," Max said in clear delight. "Amazing. Ellen, you have to try this."

"Will it hurt my babies?" Ellen asked.

"No, you will be perfectly safe," Camryn said. "Congratulations, by the way. Did you say babies?"

"We're having twins in March," Max said, walking over to his wife. He grasped her hand and pulled her from the two-seater. "Let Camryn put the patch on you. It doesn't hurt. I can't even feel it now that the thing is in place."

"The child should have one," Amme said. "Do I have your

permission to put one on him?"

"Sure. Go ahead," Max said.

Ry prowled toward Amme with the child still clinging to his back. She scooped him up and grinned at him. "Did you enjoy the ride?" she asked in careful English.

"Yes, more." He attempted to wriggle free, but Ry stepped back and shifted.

"If anyone tells the crew, I'll be forced to think up a gruesome punishment," Ry said immediately.

"You didn't enjoy being a horsey?" Camryn asked, her lips quivering as she applied the patch behind Ellen's ear.

Amme did the same with Luke and kneeled in front of him to strike up a conversation. He resembled his father and Camryn in appearance with black hair, but his bright blue eyes came from his mother. The females would love him when he was older.

"No," Ry snapped, making his feelings very clear on the topic with one crisp denial. "You have a visitor. They're pulling up outside."

"I don't hear..." Max peered out the window. "You're right. It's our neighbor, Marcus Polo. He moved in not long after you left."

"Pretend we're not home," Ellen said. "We can't introduce them to these people."

Camryn growled low in her throat, and Ellen squeaked. She backed up rapidly and gaped at Camryn, her hands wrapped around her bulging middle.

"We don't intend to harm anyone," Ry said. "We're here for a holiday and to give Camryn a chance to make her peace with you. That is all. We do not want an interstellar incident."

"Max," Ellen said.

"Don't be silly, Ellen. It will be all right," Max said. "Camryn is my sister." He left the room to answer the knock on the door.

The low rumble of masculine voices drifted down the passage.

"Amme, you need to change your color," Camryn warned.

"Oops." Amme glanced at Ellen and changed her skin to the same golden skin tone.

"Nice," Camryn said. "I should turn that color after a few visits to the beach."

"If you hurt Max." Ellen clenched and unclenched her hands even as her lips trembled. "If you hurt him or our son or me, I'll...I'll report you to the authorities."

"They won't believe you," Ry said. "They'll call you crazy."

The color fled Ellen's cheeks, leaving her pallid. Amme took a step toward her, concerned for the other woman, but halted at her wide-eyed terror.

"Not that we intend to hurt you," Camryn said. "We're here for a visit. We want to spend Christmas and New Year here then we're leaving for Viros."

"W-where is your spaceship?" Ellen stammered.

"It's hidden," Ry said. "We don't want trouble or any attention from the authorities. I promised Camryn we'd bring her home for a visit. She was worried about her brother, about all of you."

And she'd wanted to make things right, Amme knew. She wanted to apologize to her twin and show him she'd changed for the better. Ellen might make this visit difficult though. She was scared, and she disapproved of Camryn. Her silent enmity worried Amme because it was in her nature to fix relationships.

Max reappeared with a tall man with brown hair. No, not brown, Amme thought when he walked in front of a window. There were strands of red and gold mixed in with the brown. Several tuffs stood up on end as if he'd dragged his hand through his hair repeatedly, and Amme ached to smooth the locks down. Her lips quirked a fraction. Well, to touch the girth of his shoulders really. The Earthman was a magnificent male specimen.

"This man," Amme whispered to Camryn. "I pick him. Who is he?"

"I don't know. He has a child with him. He might be married."

27

Amme blinked. The man had commanded her full attention. She hadn't noticed the child holding his hand. Disappointment seared through her, followed quickly by her normal practicality. Early days yet. She had several Earth weeks to find a suitable male.

The child was a female—tiny with delicate features and the same coloring as the man. There was an air about her—one of loss that fired Amme's empathy.

"Marcus," Ellen said.

"I'm sorry," Marcus said, his husky voice pulling a visceral response from Amme. "You have visitors. I don't want to interrupt. I'll go and leave you—"

"No!" Ellen said quickly.

"Stay," Max agreed. "This is my twin sister, Camryn."

"Pleased to meet you," Camryn said, extending her hand. "This is my husband, Ry Coppersmith, and my best friend, Amme Vanak."

"Camryn," Marcus said.

"Good afternoon," Ry said, and he grinned at Camryn's imperceptible nod and followed suit by shaking hands.

Amme offered her hand next. Such a quaint Earth custom, even if it did pass on germs and bacteria. "Pleased to meet you."

Camryn winked at her, so Amme knew she'd managed her English well.

"Would you like a cup of tea?" Ellen asked.

"Why don't I make it?" Camryn said. "Amme can help me. You have a seat and relax."

Ellen cast a quick glance at Ry and retreated to a seat on the other side of the room.

Amme followed Camryn from the room, fascinated by the human kitchen. "Show me how these things work," she said. "This is so much fun."

"Hopefully my cottage is vacant so some of us can move in there," Camryn said. "Then I can teach you more stuff. We can get a Christmas tree."

Amme grinned. "Yes. You told me how to make tea. Let me see if I remember."

By the time they returned to the lounge room, Amme was proud of her accomplishments.

Unseen by his mother, Luke walked up to Ry and tugged on his hand. "Where is the kitty?"

"He went outside," Ry said, his words careful and perfect English. It was better to practice the local language rather than rely on the translators.

Amme set the tray down and let Camryn do the honors. She was looking forward to tasting tea. She'd already sneaked a piece of shortbread and found the buttery biscuit exquisite. There was shortbread with chocolate chips too. She'd try a piece of that next.

"She delivered her by courier?" The disbelief in Ellen's voice grabbed Amme's attention.

"Yes," Marcus said. "I'm not sure what to do next."

"You're keeping her." Max glanced at the child and lowered his voice. "Are you sure she's yours?"

"I'll have a DNA test done, but I'm fairly certain," Marcus said in his husky voice.

Amme continued to listen to the huddled conversation while Ry entertained the two children. Luke was brave and confident and full of childish swagger. The little girl looked as if she'd been crying, and Amme went to her, drawn by her diffident manner and the core of sorrow she wasn't old enough to hide.

She crouched beside the child. "Hello."

The girl looked at her with her big brown eyes, reticent in her response.

Amme didn't mind. Over the years she'd tended many children. She knew about patience. She smiled. "Would you like a biscuit?"

"Yes, please." She glanced at her father and leaned closer to whisper. "You talk funny."

Amme burst out laughing. "I'm not from around here."

"Me neither."

"What is your name?" Amme spoke carefully to make sure she used the correct words and gave them the right weight.

"Autumn Polo," the child said.

"I am Amme." Amme held out her hand, and Autumn wrapped her fingers around hers. Luke took her other hand, and Amme escorted them over to Camryn who handed them a piece of chocolate chip shortbread each.

"Over here, Luke," Ellen said, her tone sharp and holding a trace of uneasiness.

Oh dear. "I'm sorry," Amme said. "I should ask first."

Max frowned at his wife. "It's fine."

"Ellen makes the best shortbread," Camryn said. "She's a first-class cook."

"What do you think, Autumn? Does it taste good?" Amme asked.

The little girl nodded.

"You're good with her," Marcus said, coming to stand beside her. "She hasn't said much to me at all. Are you used to children?"

"Yes, I've looked after several children. Childcare is my job." His voice did things to her—strummed her nerve endings and her tronic receptors, transmitted messages at ultra-speed through her hidden enhancements. She dragged in a quick breath and his scent filled her senses. He smelled enticing.

"I don't suppose you'd be interested in helping out with Autumn? Children are a mystery to me, and I could do with some help. I'd pay you well."

"She's not a suitable—" Ellen said.

Amme cut her off. "I'd love to, but I'm only here for the holiday period."

"This isn't a good idea." Ellen raised her chin in defiance.

"Camryn," Max said. "What do you think?"

"Amme has lots of experience with children, but this is up to her. She's here on holiday. We were going to the beach and shopping," Camryn said.

"I'll pay extra," Marcus said quickly. "I'm desperate, and I live at the next door property, so Amme won't be far away."

"I'll do it," Amme said and winked at Camryn.

"But you should check on references," Ellen said.

"Ellen." Max's voice held a warning.

"I'm desperate," Marcus said, and his charming grin and beseeching gaze continued to work their magic on Amme. "I need help."

This man was fling material. "I'll help," Amme said, her English coming more easily. "No problem."

Marcus liked the tall woman's confidence. He liked her easy smile and her manner with Autumn. Used to thinking on his feet and making decisive decisions, he had a good feeling about Amme Vanak. Of course, it didn't hurt she was a pretty woman with long black hair and eyes the color of his favorite Scottish whisky. An attractive package, yet she wasn't flirting with him or trading on her looks. That made him decide to employ her despite Ellen's caution.

"Can you come with me now?" he asked.

Amme glanced at Camryn and Ry, then turned back to him with a nod. "Yes."

"Thank you." Talk about lucking out.

"We'll deliver your bag for you," Camryn said.

Marcus smiled at Amme. "We can take it now."

"It's still at our hotel," Camryn said. "We'll drop it by later tonight." She turned to Max. "I was hoping my cottage was empty. Ry and I wouldn't mind crashing there, maybe with some of our friends."

"How many are there?" Marcus asked, wondering where Amme

SHELLEY MUNRO

came from. She had a bit of an accent, one he couldn't place, despite having traveled the world.

"We have five other friends traveling with us," Camryn said.

"I have a guest cottage," Marcus said. "If your friends don't mind sharing bedrooms, there will be plenty of room for all of them."

"That's incredibly generous," Camryn said. "Are you sure? We're not leaving until the beginning of the new year."

Marcus smiled, his gaze on Amme. Still no sign of flirtation, and he felt interest tugging him. *Not this woman.* She was a friend of Max's sister and out of bounds. "It's the least I can do since Amme has volunteered to help me with Autumn."

"They're already in a hotel," Ellen began.

"Ellen," Max said. "We should make a fresh pot of tea." He grasped his wife's arm and guided her from the room.

Luke shot straight to Ry and grasped his hand. "We need to find kitty. Give him some milk to drink."

"No, sweetie," Camryn said, devilment making an appearance. "The kitty is busy right now."

"Is Ellen all right?" Marcus asked. "She seems a bit off today." There was a weird tension in the atmosphere, or maybe it was him, out of step because of Autumn's arrival.

His mind darted to his parents, and his breath whistled through his teeth. His mother would shit a brick when she discovered her new grandmother status. Traditional in the seen-but-not-heard vein, she was a woman who hadn't expected to have children. Both he and Olivia were mistakes, and she hadn't given nature an opportunity to upset her life a third time. A medical procedure had taken care of that, and carefully chosen employees had brought up her children. These days his parents traveled extensively and spent much of their time in Europe. The best solution for all concerned parties.

"Our fault," Camryn said, some of the brightness departing

32

her demeanor. "I'm afraid we've sprung ourselves on her unexpectedly. We'll drop off our friends and Amme's bags in a few hours. Is that okay?"

"That's fine," Marcus said. "They'll need to stock the fridge. Everything else is in the cupboards—the bedding and towels."

"No prob. Ry and I will grab some groceries."

Amme frowned. "But—"

"I'll take you shopping tomorrow," Camryn promised, obviously anticipating Amme's objection. "I presume you'll need to stock up on stuff for Autumn. Amme and I can get a few basics tomorrow."

Marcus gave a rueful shrug. Women and shopping. Maybe Amme wasn't so different after all. "I hadn't even thought that far ahead."

"We should go," Amme said. "Autumn looks exhausted."

"Good call." The kid was drooping and wavering on her feet. Marcus scooped up his daughter and glanced at Amme. "I can't thank you enough for helping."

"I'll walk out with you," Camryn said.

Max and Ellen returned with another pot of tea. Ellen bore evidence of weeping. Just as well they were leaving. Autumn's tears were bad enough. He didn't want to cope with a weeping pregnant woman too.

"We're off. The kid is almost asleep," Marcus said.

"Okay. Let me get the door," Max said.

Camryn dragged Amme away and they did a lot of whispering. More secrets. Marcus wondered if he should search for hidden cameras. Hell of a day.

Camryn glanced at Marcus then started whispering instructions. "Contact me via your ear com if you run into any problems or need to ask a question. I'll get Mogens to bring more translators, just in case. It will be easy enough to put one on Autumn, but you're going to need to get creative with Marcus. It's possible he won't need a translator. You've practiced your English. Just follow the plan and tell anyone who asks you're from Romania. We don't know Marcus. It's best not to give him info that could cause trouble. I'll come and pick you and Autumn up tomorrow. We'll do some shopping and maybe hit the beach."

"He said he will pay me. Will I be able to use that for shopping?" Amme asked.

Camryn had taught them a lot, so they'd manage to blend, but this wasn't something that had come up in their varied discussions.

"You won't get paid until you've worked for a week. Don't worry. I have my credit cards and money in my account. It's not as if I'll need it on Viros. Don't forget. If you require anything, com me."

Amme climbed into the passenger seat of the Earth vehicle and remembered to click on her safety harness. She scanned the controls and the instrument panels with one comprehensive gaze, her cortex enhancement gathering and storing intel. Marcus started up the vehicle, and she waved at Camryn and Ry. Some of her ennui had faded since their arrival. This was an adventure, and she couldn't wait to experience more.

CHAPTER THREE

"Where do you come from, Amme?"

"A small village in Romania," Amme said promptly. Change the subject. "What do you do?"

"My family is involved in travel and tourism, but I've branched into import and export of foodstuffs, mainly exotic spices," Marcus said. "Recently, I've dabbled in imports and exports for the interior decorating trade."

"I see," Amme said, giving one of the answers Camryn had suggested if she didn't quite understand. "That must be...challenging." Yes, that was the right word.

"Not as tough as a surprise child," Marcus said drily.

He turned the vehicle up a long driveway bordered by trees with scarlet flowers. White fences kept animals from wandering onto the road. They drove around a curve, and Amme caught her first glimpse of a huge, sprawling house.

"It's beautiful."

"I like it," Marcus said. "I enjoy the peace and quiet after the noise of my city apartment. That's the cottage where your friends will stay."

"It's big."

"That's what my mother says. She tells me this place is too large for one person."

Marcus stopped the vehicle and handed her a set of keys. "I'll get Autumn if you could open the front door for me."

"Yes," Amme said.

She trotted to the door and managed to open it with the third key she tried. The small victory made her want to do a little dance.

"Should I take Autumn to a bedroom?" he asked.

"Yes, she needs to recharge, ah...sleep," Amme said.

She followed Marcus along a passage and up a set of stairs, taking the opportunity to gaze at him from behind. He wore a jacket and matching trews. Trousers, Amme corrected. He wore a suit. Yes, that was it. His legs were long, and he had a fit appearance, much like Ry. She'd enjoy seeing him with fewer clothes to judge if he had muscle tone similar to Camryn's mate. Her internal heart-pump started pulsating at a rapid rate. Amme, stilled, frowned then hurried to catch up.

He turned into a big bedroom with two beds. "I think this is the best room for Autumn. It has an en suite. I'll put you in the bedroom right next door."

"Does she have more clothes?"

"Yes. Her bag is still in the car. I'll get it now." He strode out, leaving her alone with Autumn. Amme's stomach flipped in an odd manner as she watched him, and she did a quick mental assessment. All her cyborg parts were functioning correctly.

Amme took the opportunity to place a translator behind Autumn's ear. She needed to understand the child at all times, and she didn't want her own language skills to get in the way. "Are you hungry?"

Autumn shook her head.

"Let's get you into bed then," Amme said and led the child into the en suite Marcus had indicated. As she'd expected, it was a sanitizer room, and she quickly washed Autumn's face and hands with real water instead of the artificial substances they used on board the *Indy*. The child used the facilities, and Amme hustled her back to bed.

"Here you go," Marcus said.

Something rang in the distance.

"I'd better get that," Marcus said. "Come and find me in the kitchen once you have her settled. I'll give you a tour and we can discuss what to have for dinner. Cooking is one thing that I can do."

Amme whipped off Autumn's T-shirt and her trews. Trousers. No, jeans, she thought after feeling the blue fabric. She opened the suitcase and found a pair of pink pajamas with weird-looking cats emblazoned on the material. There was also a pink animal. When it didn't move or attempt communication, Amme picked it up, using caution in case the animal was playing dead and bit her.

"Teddy." Autumn reached for the animal without fear, and Amme handed it over. Maybe it was one of those toys Camryn had mentioned.

The child fell silent while Amme dressed her. She slid into one of the beds and was asleep before Amme tucked the covers around her small form.

Amme took a moment to unpack the bag and familiarize herself with Autumn's possessions. A tiny brush for the teeth. Ah, one step she'd forgotten. Time for that tomorrow.

Pleased and excited, she explored. More bedrooms. Ah, Marcus's bedroom. The room smelled like Marcus, and her tronic receptors spiked, sending messages of more than friendly interest to her brain. Those messages transmitted to her heart-pump, and her stomach tingled. Amme frowned. That had never happened before when she'd picked a male for intimacy reasons.

In the past, her vitals had remained even without a spike or blip in performance.

Her mind went straight to the horrors of malfunction. No! She couldn't go offline now. She'd miss most of the holiday.

Marcus was the perfect Earthman for her to experience a sexual exchange.

Now, what had Camryn said? Yes, she had to express her interest with subtle signs. This was how it was done on Earth, although Camryn had mentioned that sometimes the direct approach was preferable. Direct was the cyborg way, but she truly would enjoy experiencing Earth's customs.

Subtle it was then.

She found Marcus in the kitchen—a huge room with appliances and gleaming surfaces in shades of black, gray, and red. Over to one side, there was a table with the same glossy black top, and a huge window let in light and allowed diners to study the view. More trees and grass and fluffy brown-and-cream animals. To her right, the bank of windows curved outward. The glass doors displayed flower gardens, a stretch of green lawn, a pool of water, and more trees. A sunny spot to while away part of the daily cycle. It must be nice, Amme thought, to sit in such a place.

"What are those animals?" she asked. "They have such long lashes." *Oops.* The sec the words left her mouth, she inwardly cringed. Her vision allowed her to see well, but most Earth people wouldn't see that far.

"Alpacas," Marcus said, giving her an odd look. "I breed them for their wool."

"Cute creatures. I like them."

Marcus grinned. "So do I. I'll take you and Autumn to visit my herd tomorrow. I have a swimming pool. It's not fenced, so you'll need to make sure Autumn doesn't go out there alone."

"I will watch her. She won't come to any harm with me."

"Would you like a glass of wine?"

"Yes, please." Camryn had mentioned wine. She'd said it was tasty and similar to the Ornum fizz, although not as strong as the beverage from the convict planet.

"White or red?"

Another decision. "I don't mind. You choose."

"I'm going to barbecue some steaks for dinner. We'll have red." He poured ruby-colored liquid into two glasses and handed her one. "Is Autumn okay? She didn't cry again?"

"She's tired, and this is a big change for her. I'll watch her closely."

"I guess we'll need a schedule or something?"

He sounded lost as a child himself. Amme found herself grinning. "A routine is good for a child." She took a sip from her glass, and a hum of appreciation escaped. "This is delicious."

"This merlot is one of my favorites." Marcus gulped a mouthful and set down his glass. "I can't believe I have a daughter."

"You didn't know?"

"Her arrival took me by surprise. No, shocked me, if you want the truth. I remember Candy. I slept with her, but we were together for a long weekend. Neither of us wanted anything permanent. She never contacted me and I thought we'd both moved on with our lives."

Amme frowned, not understanding some of his terms. *Keep it simple.* Camryn's voice whispered through her mind—a reminder to speak in short sentences. "She died."

"Yes. I checked on the net. Candice Kane died last week."

"Do you want me to help with dinner?"

"No, I've got this. I need something to do to keep busy. Gotta figure out how to tell my folks, my next move. Need a plan."

"Sometimes plans are not necessary. It's almost Christmas holidays."

"You think I should take time off work and have a holiday?" He drank some of his wine. "I can't remember the last time I had one."

"You're not working now."

"No. Where in Romania do you come from?"

"A small village. I haven't lived there for a long time." *Like never.* "I...it was a bad period of my life, and I don't like to talk...remember." She took a sip of her wine and then another.

"More wine?"

"Please," Amme said. "It tastes very good. You should have a Christmas tree."

Marcus cocked his head, and his lips curled upward in a smile that made her gape. "I've never had a tree before. Mum and Dad always go away for Christmas. My sister and I and our nanny used to go with them when we were younger."

"And now?"

"It's just another day, one that I work from home instead of going into the office. Or..." He slid her a repentant glance. "I'd spend the day with a girlfriend."

"You have a child now."

Marcus bowed his shoulders and resembled someone bearing a heavy weight. "That's what worries me. I don't know how to do any of this stuff. I don't want to take after my parents. I want to do this right."

Amme placed her fingers over the top of his in silent commiseration. "You will do a fine job." The warmth from his skin seeped into her own cooler flesh. A breath caught halfway up her throat, and a sort of a lump formed. She coughed, and the blockage moved. She shifted her hand and did a quick internal reading of her sensors.

No, nothing seemed out of order.

Well, that was weird.

Marcus didn't say anything for a long time, merely drank more of his wine.

"Camryn promised us a special Christmas like the ones she used to have when she was little. You should share our celebration."

"I'd like that. I need to go into the office tomorrow." He paused, and his brow wrinkled.

Amme reached out to soothe the worry lines, and when she realized what she was doing, she let her hand drop back to her side.

He nodded as if he'd come to a decision. "There are a few things I'll need to take care of, but I can work here at the farm instead of at the office."

"I hear a vehicle," Amme said.

Marcus walked to a window and glanced out. "You have good hearing. I didn't hear a thing. It's your friends." He grabbed a set of keys off a hook. "I'll show them the cottage."

"I'll check on Autumn." Amme glanced at Marcus, and her receptors jumped, transmitting messages to her brain control she couldn't decipher. Peculiar. She needed to discuss this with Camryn. Maybe it was Earth's atmosphere.

Autumn was asleep and curled up in a ball. Tight and protected, Amme thought. Poor child. It would take time for Autumn and Marcus to become used to each other, but they'd make it and become a family.

"Amme? Where are you?" Camryn called.

Amme sped down the stairs. "Shush, don't make such a racket." It was a relief not to focus on her English. "Autumn is asleep."

"Sorry," Camryn said, her voice softer. "Marcus told me to come inside. Here's your bag."

"Thanks." Amme took the bag Camryn handed her. "Come and see my room. It's beautiful."

"The entire house is gorgeous," Camryn said.

"I wonder if I should stay. There seems to be something wrong with my receptors. Here keeps tingling." She cupped her hand over one breast. "My internal heart-pump is going too fast. And my stomach feels funny. It's the same feeling I get when I'm confronted with a child who needs me, but it's much, much stronger whenever I'm with Marcus. I think I'm malfunctioning."

Camryn's lips moved in an odd tremor. "What were you doing when this feeling started?"

"I looked at Marcus, and the second time, I touched his hand. Camryn, do you think it can be fixed? I don't want to go offline for internal diagnostics. That would make me miss most of our holiday. I like Autumn. I like Marcus." She shivered when her thoughts drifted to him, her heart-pump banging hard.

"Ah," Camryn said, and the corners of her mouth turned up into a broad smirk. "I think Marcus is the perfect man for a fling."

"Why are you laughing at me?"

"That feeling you describe is sexual attraction. You're attracted to Marcus, and this is your body's way of showing you."

"You don't get this with Ry."

"Yes, I do. Every time he smiles or touches me. My knees go weak. My heart beats faster. You told me when you are with a male, your body responds to stimulation. Your symptoms are the initial signs of stimulation. They're normal."

Amme frowned, trying to make sense of Camryn's explanation. "But I have never felt this before."

"Because the males you've spent time with might have given you sexual pleasure, but they didn't move your heart."

"I don't understand," Amme said.

"Don't worry." Camryn gave her a quick hug, and a sense of acceptance spread through Amme.

"I feel a response when you hug me. It's not as strong but still similar."

"You say the sweetest things." Camryn squeezed her arm. "You're feeling familial love. We—the crew of the Indy—are a family. I feel the same for all the crew members, but the feeling for Ry is much deeper and stronger."

Confusion filled Amme. She tried to understand but needed

more information to comprehend. "So it is all right to like Marcus this way?"

"As long as you remember we're leaving in the new year. You don't want a broken heart."

"My heart-pump is indestructible. It is designed not to break and will continue to augment the one I was born with. It gives me extra strength."

Camryn linked her arm with Amme's. "Let's go and catch up with the rest of the crew. It's good that they'll be close. Don't worry about this stuff. Just enjoy spending time with Marcus."

"Your words make sense."

"Good."

They walked down the stairs and tromped outside, Camryn leading the way to the cottage Marcus had pointed out when they arrived.

"Are you and Ry staying with your brother?"

"Yes, my stuff is still in the cottage."

"Your sister doesn't like you," Amme said.

"My sister-in-law," Camryn corrected. "No, she doesn't trust me. I understand her attitude and expected it. Max is my twin. We've always had each other's back, but I hurt Max, and I put Luke in danger. Ellen can't forgive me for that. I need to regain her trust."

"You are not upset?"

"A little. I hope I can fix this before we leave. I'm going to try."

"Amme, there you are." Gweneth's pretty face blazed with pleasure, and the salve hid the cat tattoo so well Amme wouldn't have suspected its presence. She wore a similar pair of jeans to Amme's and a sleeveless tunic top that picked out the green of her eyes, the new clothing replicator they'd purchased an excellent investment.

"Is everyone here?" Amme asked.

Gweneth nodded. "Mogens is in the garden." She lowered her

voice. "He wanted to feel the energy and do a cloud reading. Marcus told him we're welcome to swim in the pool and play a game called tennis. We can walk in the gardens any time we want." She spun around, excitement bringing a hint of pink to her cheeks while her black hair fanned out with each turn.

"Steady, Gweneth," Amme murmured. "We don't want to attract unwanted attention."

Gweneth glanced over her shoulder. "It's only us. Marcus is helping Ry and Nanu with the luggage."

"Marcus said we can get a Christmas tree," Amme said, showing some excitement of her own. Her heart-pump lurched a little crazily. The Earthman again, but this time, she knew to expect the variance. "Maybe we could get two and have one in here too. We must consult with Camryn."

"Consult with me about what?" Camryn asked.

"Christmas trees. One for the house and one for here," Amme said.

Camryn nodded. "Tomorrow."

"I'd better get back to the house in case Autumn wakes up," Amme said. "I will com you later."

"We can discuss our shopping trip," Camryn said. "Jannike and Kaya want to come with us."

"Me too," Gweneth said.

"We're going to hire a van so we can all fit," Camryn said.

"I'll com you later to say good night," Gweneth said.

Amme shot a quick glance toward Marcus who was chatting with Nanu and Jannike. "My com will be on vibrate. Leave a message if I don't answer straightaway."

Amme's friends were friendly and boisterous, and occasionally, they lapsed into a strange series of clicks and grunts that resembled none of the foreign languages he'd heard. He was pretty sure it wasn't Romania's national language.

"When did you fly in?" he asked.

"Late morning." Jannike, the tall, blonde Amazon-like woman answered. She sported a plaster on her forehead, and one of her eyes appeared slightly bruised.

"Ry and I are going back to the farm," Camryn said. "Thanks again for letting us use your cottage."

"Amme is the one doing me a big favor. It's no problem."

Camryn waved, and Ry took her arm, steering her from the cottage. "See you tomorrow."

Marcus glanced around for Amme. "Where's Amme?"

"She has gone back to the house," Kaya said.

Marcus tried not to stare, but her hair was a weird color between bright blue and black. Women did the strangest things with their appearance. "Are you all set? Do you need anything?"

Jannike spoke, but it was in those weird and rapid clicks and grunts.

"English," Nanu said, his tone sharp and his elbow equally treacherous because Jannike let out a manly oomph.

"Sorry. We are fine." Jannike rubbed her ribs and glared at her friend. "Thank you."

"Good night," Marcus said.

He found Amme in the kitchen. "Are your friends from Romania too?"

Her quick look held sharpness before it smoothed to a sexy smile. "No, we're not from the same place. Autumn is still asleep."

"Should we wake her for dinner?"

"No. She should recharge...I mean sleep."

"I'll go and heat the barbecue for the steaks. Would you start the salad? My personal shopper made sure the fridge was stocked."

Amme nodded and moved to the fridge. As he left to turn on the barbecue, he thought he heard her muttering under her breath. Damn, he didn't want to upset her.

"I can make the salad," he said.

"No! I make," Amme said, her back still to him.

When he returned, she'd opened a bag of salad leaves and tipped them into a bowl. Tomatoes, olives, cheese, and red onion sat beside a chopping board. She was muttering under her breath.

"You talk to yourself," he said.

She let out a soft eep and whirled around a vegetable knife aimed toward his gut. Immediately, she relaxed and set the knife on the counter. "You creep. Make noise next time."

Marcus barked out a laugh. "I can get bells to wear. I came back for the steaks. I think there's some garlic bread. We'll have some of that too." He went to the fridge and found the garlic bread. He pulled out a green cucumber. "I like cucumber in my salad."

He'd heat the foil-wrapped garlic bread on the barbecue. Might as well use the thing. He didn't think he'd used it more than a handful of times since he purchased it.

With the steaks on the grill and the bread heating under the hood, he wandered back to the kitchen, whistling this time. Amme was staring at the cucumber as if she'd never seen one before. "I'll peel it," he said.

"I have not had this before," she said.

"I think there are some croutons in the pantry. Grab the canister, will you? Might as well use the things since the personal shopper bought them."

"You don't like to shop?"

"I don't have time," Marcus said. "Would you like another glass of wine?"

"Yes, please." Amme walked toward the pantry, and he heard low muttering again. She sure talked to herself a lot. She disappeared into the pantry and reappeared after a long moment holding the croutons.

"Did you get lost in there?"

"No. I was checking your supplies for breakfast cereals and eggs. You don't have any. Autumn needs a nu-nutritious breakfast." She stumbled over some of her words, and he had difficulty holding a grin at bay. She was dang cute, and still, she hadn't tried to flirt with him.

"Make me a list and I'll do an online grocery order after we eat. They'll deliver tomorrow."

She nodded. "I check on Autumn."

Marcus grinned, a full out, unconcealed grin as she scuttled from the room. *This woman is your nanny. You do not need to mess with her.* Yet, he couldn't help watching the sway of her hips and her long legs and curvy butt, outlined by tight denim. The woman was gorgeous and full of sex appeal. Any one of his friends would have hit on her by now. Damn, he wanted to in the worst way.

"Still asleep," Amme said. "I made a list." She tapped her forehead.

"Paper and pen in the drawer. Back in a sec." He went out to check the steaks. Perfect. He put them on plates, grabbed the garlic bread, and toted them back inside. "Knives, forks in that drawer," he said. "Can you bring the salad?"

"I do not need to write a list," she said. "I have superior memory."

"Okay." His lips quirked. "You can help me with the order after dinner."

Amme placed the cutlery and the salad on the table. Marcus topped up their wineglasses.

"I usually eat by myself or grab takeaway."

She frowned as if she didn't understand.

"Chinese or Indian food. They're my favorites. Sometimes I get pizza."

She nodded.

"Some salad?"

She frowned again. "Yes, please." She stared at him, her gaze skimming his hair and other features to land on his lips.

The air whooshed from Marcus's lungs, and every single bit of blood roared south, leaving him lightheaded and breathless. She blinked, a slow bat of eyelashes, and glanced at the salad. Oh yeah. Salad. He sucked in a quick breath and used a pair of tongs to place salad on her plate.

"Bread?"

"It smells funny."

"That's the garlic," he said, pleased to have something else to concentrate on instead of fighting the urge to stare at her like an uncouth youth. "Have you not tried garlic bread before?"

"No."

"Try a piece. You don't have to finish it if the bread isn't to your taste." He opened the foil while he spoke and tore off a piece. He handed it to her and grabbed two slices for himself. He added salad to his plate and willed himself to behave. "What's the verdict on the bread?"

She chewed and swallowed, which would have been fine, but the shiny smear of butter at the corner of her mouth almost did him in. Hell, he usually controlled himself better. What was it about this woman that drove him crazy? His cock was almost full mast, and his trouser fabric fought the expansion. He shifted in his seat, but it didn't make a blind bit of difference.

"It's very tasty," she said and took another bite.

The smear of butter remained, and he couldn't help himself.

"You have some butter…" He reached over and used his thumb to stroke away the smear. "That's better."

She studied him, seemingly frozen by the physical contact, and he silently cursed himself. Damn, he'd frightened her. He shot her another look and caught her gaze. Her whiskey eyes glowed with a weird inner light. He blinked, and when he checked again, they appeared normal.

"I want to kiss you," she blurted.

Marcus gaped because she hadn't shown a single indication of being aware of him as a man. "Yes," he said, and his voice emerged in an unmanly croak.

Her forehead wrinkled. "You want this?"

"Yes, but I don't want to mess things up between us. I need your help with Autumn."

"Autumn is a sweetie. I will not leave you until my holiday ends. This, I promise. It is not in my nature to break my vows."

Marcus stared again, nonplussed by her words and by the certainty and determination inherent in them. This woman was odd, but in a good way. It was clear she held strong values. No. No, he couldn't mess this up. "I don't think kissing is appropriate."

Her brows rose. "I repulse you?"

"No, not at all. It's more important for me to focus on Autumn." Marcus meant it. This wasn't a line spun to get a woman in bed. He cut a piece of steak and popped it into his mouth.

She nodded. "Camryn explained this to me. We will get to know each other first, then you can kiss me, and we will have sex."

Marcus almost choked. He managed to swallow and reached for his wine, taking a big gulp while he gawked at Amme.

"Did I say something wrong? Do you not want to kiss me or have sex with me? I have been told I am very good at sex."

Marcus's mouth worked, but his brain didn't. The words he wanted to say didn't transmit. Somehow, he'd lost control of the situation.

"Marcus? Do you not want this?"

He wanted to laugh. His cock was so hard he suspected it would bear zipper marks. What he wanted was to haul Amme off to bed. "I w-would—" She'd reduced him to stutters. Him. One of the most powerful businessmen in the southern hemisphere. He cleared his throat and tried again. "I want this, but we will go at my pace." His words emerged in a stern growl.

"Yes, Marcus." Amme picked up her knife and fork and began to cut her steak. She ate with ladylike manners. "Autumn will require more clothes. Camryn says we will go to the beach. She will need a swimsuit."

Marcus blinked but decided to go with the subject change. Maybe a discussion of clothes and his daughter would reduce the swelling of his cock.

"I'll give you a credit card to make purchases for Autumn."

"Can I buy a Christmas tree?"

"I can arrange that," Marcus said.

"Can we buy one for the cottage too?"

"Yes. You'll need to purchase decorations. Camryn will know the best place to get those."

"I like this garlic bread."

"How is the steak?"

"Okay. I enjoy the salad better."

Marcus paused. "Are you a vegetarian?"

"My system likes vegetables better."

Her system? That was an odd way of putting it. "We'll order extra vegetables then."

Once they'd finished dinner Amme went to check on Autumn, her diligence and concern for his daughter impressing the hell out of him. Of course, it was early days, but he thought he'd lucked out. It was a shame she'd leave, but depending on how things went, maybe he could persuade Amme to stay when her friends left.

Amme returned and helped him clean up the kitchen.

"You don't have to help," he said. "Go and relax in the lounge."

"No, I like to feel useful," she said.

"I'm just rinsing the dishes and putting them in the dishwasher."

"Show me," Amme said. "I want to learn."

"All right," Marcus said. Maybe they didn't have dishwashers where she came from. "You stand the plates up in this section. Knives and forks here. Glasses and cups here. Pots here. Where did you and your friends fly in from?"

"I've decided to buy a bikini. That will allow more skin to show.

Camryn said it is not proper to go naked in public here."

The dish Marcus had picked up slid from between his fingers. It hit the counter and bounced on the floor before smashing.

"Oh, it's broken," Amme said.

"Don't move. I'll get a broom," Marcus said and scurried away to the utility room.

This woman was going to drive him into Crazy town. Now that she'd mentioned naked, he couldn't get the vision his imagination conjured out of his mind.

Naked.

Yes, please.

His hand bore a noticeable tremor when he reached for the broom. With the dustpan in hand, he strode back to the kitchen to find Amme carefully picking up the larger pieces.

"If you cut yourself, I'm going to put you over my knee and spank you," Marcus snapped. "I told you not to move."

"Oh, I enjoy spanking," Amme said. "It fires my receptors and makes the sex really good."

The broom slipped through his fingers and hit the floor. He glared at Amme. "Stop talking." Hell's bells. The erection that had finally subsided took on new life, and Marcus sighed inwardly. No doubt about it. Amme was going to give his willpower a real workout.

CHAPTER FOUR

Amme glanced at Autumn. She seemed happy enough in her car seat. She was sitting beside Gweneth, and the two were conversing. Perfect because Gweneth was too young to hear what she wanted to discuss with Camryn and the others.

"He threatened to spank me," Amme blurted, no longer able to hold in the information.

"What?" Jannike asked.

"No," Kaya said and clapped her hands together.

"How did the subject come up?" Camryn demanded. "Damn thing. Get in gear."

A horrid crunch came from the engine.

"Let me do it before you break our transport," Amme said. "You're the person who was born on this planet. I thought you could work their machines. Which position do you want?"

"One," Camryn said. "My foot is on the clutch now. I used to drive automatic vehicles."

Amme reached over and slid the gear into the correct position. She was good at retaining information. Once she heard instructions, she never forgot.

"I told him I wanted to kiss him," Amme said.

The van hopped once before Camryn managed to get it working. "Was that before or after I told you how to make a salad?"

"After. We had this stuff called garlic bread. He wiped some food off my mouth. He looked as if he wanted to kiss me, so I gave him permission."

"Not quite the same thing," Kaya said and tucked a strand of hair behind her ear.

"Your ear is showing," Jannike said. "It still looks pointy to me."

Kaya wrinkled her pert nose and rearranged her hair. "Tell us what happened."

"Nothing," Amme said, still disappointed. "Autumn woke during the night and screamed. I was in with her, trying to calm her down. She said there were monsters hiding in the wardrobe. I was checking for monsters and doing a go-monster spell when Marcus walked into the bedroom. He took one look at me and got this weird expression as if he were in severe pain."

"What were you wearing?" Camryn asked.

"No, more to the point, what was he wearing?" Jannike asked.

"I had on a T-shirt and my jeans," Amme said.

"Bad move," Kaya said. "We need to get her some of that Earth lingerie stuff today. First stop."

"And a swimsuit. I told him I was going to get a bikini, but usually, I didn't wear anything when I was swimming."

Camryn barked out a laugh at the same time as she changed gear, ready to turn onto the main road. The van jumped forward in a series of jerky hops.

"That does it," Amme said. "Describe the road rules and the van controls so I can drive us back home. We have a child in this vehicle.

I favor the idea of lingerie."

"I hope you have plenty of currency," Jannike said to Camryn. "I want some of this lingerie stuff too."

Amme had never had such a fun day, and they arrived back at Marcus's house with lots of parcels. Even Autumn was laughing and happily chattering with the other women.

"When are we going to the beach?" Autumn asked.

"We've run out of time today, but we can have a swim in the pool," Amme said.

"I can't swim," the child said. "I can float and started to learn to paddle like a dog."

"I'll teach you," Camryn said.

Amme pulled up in front of the house. "Let's unload everything here and sort out our packages inside. I'll make coffee."

"Ooh, listen to Amme," Kaya said to Jannike. "The lady hostess."

"No biscuits for you," Amme said. "We have some. We ordered chocolate chip cookies on the internet last night." She climbed out and opened the rear door to let Autumn out of her car seat.

"I want to try some more of that chocolate stuff," Kaya said.

"Me too," Jannike said.

"God," Camryn muttered. "I thought the shop owner was going to have a coronary when you two started eating all her samples."

"She offered them to us," Kaya said.

Camryn chuckled. "True, but next time just take one, not a handful."

The other women clambered out of the van and divvied up the parcels.

Amme led Autumn into the kitchen and sat her at the kitchen counter. "You wait there while I help the others with the packages."

Autumn nodded. "I want a swim."

"As soon as we get organized," Amme promised. "And we have to blow up the wings to help you float."

"I didn't realize we'd purchased so many things," Camryn said.

"Will it be all right?" Jannike asked. "You have enough currency?"

"My first husband had a lot of money," Camryn said. "Gabriel had it invested and the interest has mounted up while I've been away. Plus there is the sale proceeds from our apartment that I sold. Luckily, I wasn't stupid enough to spend all my money when I was drunk."

"Lucky for us," Amme said, giving Camryn a one-armed hug. "Thank you for sharing your currency with us."

Camryn shrugged. "You're my family. Besides, it's not as if I'm going to get back to Earth very often."

And it was true. They were a family. They might bicker and tease each other, but if any one of them required help it wasn't necessary to ask. "Until Gweneth and I joined the Indy, I'd never had a family," Amme said. "It makes my heart-pump swell."

"Your heart," Camryn said with a smile. "It makes your heart full."

"Enough with the mushy stuff," Jannike said in her usual tough manner. "I need to eat then I want to see what happens to my new swimsuit when it gets wet." She held up a tiny suit, and doubt furrowed her brow as she scowled at the bright orange-and-black fabric. "I was surprised it fit me."

Amme shared a glance with Camryn, and they both laughed.

"I'll teach you how to make sandwiches," Camryn said. "A skill everyone should learn."

"I can make sandwiches," Autumn said.

"Perfect," Amme said. "You can show me how. What do we need first?"

"Chocolate," Kaya said, searching through all her packages.

"Ah!" She seized a wrapped bar from amongst the shopping bags. "Do I eat the wrapping?"

Camryn studied the ceiling, puffed out a breath. "Damn, I'm so tempted. No, can't do it," she muttered. "No, you rip it open. I can show—"

"I'll do it," Kaya said, taking an abrupt step back. She peeled the wrapper back of a large chocolate bar and took a big bite.

"See all those small squares," Camryn said.

"Yeth," Kaya said through a mouthful of dark chocolate. She swallowed and moaned her pleasure.

"The squares are there to help break off pieces," Camryn said. "So that it's easy to share."

"Oh." Kaya pulled back the wrapper and broke off individual squares. "One for you. One for you." She dispensed single squares until everyone had one.

Jannike popped hers into her mouth. "Thank you so much for sharing."

Camryn grinned and accepted her allocation.

"That's not going to fill us up." Amme ate her single square before Kaya demanded it back. "We definitely need sandwiches. What do we do first, Autumn?"

The sandwich-making lesson took no time, and soon, they moved out to the pool, all dressed in their new swimwear.

"Camryn, how does this flutter board work?" Amme asked.

"I'll show you now." Camryn pulled off her T-shirt to reveal her bright red bikini.

Amme led Autumn to the pool.

"This is a pretty suit," Autumn said. "I like blue."

"I know," Amme said, her voice grave while her heart-pump did an extra little squeeze. "You told us blue is your favorite color."

"I can float," Autumn said again.

"Really? You'd better show me, so I can learn." Amme listened to Camryn's explanation about holding her breath and kicking, and watched both Camryn and Autumn float in the shallow end of the pool.

Gweneth, Jannike, and Kaya splashed and tossed around a ball at the other end of the pool.

"Someone is coming," Camryn said and waded from the pool. "Two vehicles." She raised her head and sniffed then relaxed. "Ry is here."

Ry appeared around the corner of the house, and Amme caught the flare of passion in his features when he saw Camryn. She sighed. That was exactly what she wanted to find one day. Unlikely, it was true, but a cyborg could hope. Living and traveling with the Indy meant her life was quite different from her original purpose. Maybe one day she'd find a man who wanted to keep her—a man like Marcus.

As if she'd summoned him, the man walked around the corner of the house with Nanu. He was listening to something Nanu said. He must have felt her gaze because he glanced over toward the pool and came to an abrupt halt. Mogens plowed into him from behind, sending Marcus lurching forward two steps.

Amme glanced down at her scantily clad body and a smirk crept into position. Job done.

"We went to the Christmas tree farm and bought two trees," Nanu said. "We have them on a trailer. And we got some mistletoe stuff, but it's not real 'cause the real stuff is rare."

"We'll unload them in a bit," Marcus said, his gaze still on Amme. She was golden skin and curves, her body in perfect proportion. He lifted his hand in acknowledgment then his attention went to his daughter. She wore a blue polka-dotted swimsuit and her hair was wet so she'd been swimming already.

"I could do with a swim," Nanu said.

"We should unload the trees first," Ry said.

"Aye, Captain," Nanu said. "I'll get the girls. It was their idea, so they should help with the hard work."

"Captain? Were you in the forces?"

"No," Ry said, and when he didn't add anything, Marcus frowned.

There was something odd about this group, something that fired his instincts. He didn't get a bad feeling, but there was something not quite normal, and he couldn't fathom what.

Nanu trotted over to the pool and spoke to the women. They levered themselves out of the pool and pulled T-shirts over their bikinis.

Marcus glanced back at Amme. She was chatting with Autumn and helping her remove her water wings. Something inside him tightened at the ease with which Amme dealt with his daughter.

"I'm so lucky Amme agreed to help me with Autumn. She's a natural."

Nanu shrugged. "She's programmed that way."

"What?" Marcus asked.

"Amme likes children," Ry said quickly. "Nanu, let's get started manhandling these trees."

Marcus spent the rest of the day watching the friends interact. Occasionally, when they thought he wasn't listening or if he left and returned to the group, he heard them communicating in those weird clicks and grunts. Then there was the enjoyment they took in setting up the trees. A small thing, but all of them—even Camryn—took a childlike pleasure in the process. Their excitement was rubbing off on him, making everything feel new and bringing back memories of times when his family actually talked and spent a day together.

"What do you think?" he asked Amme and Autumn.

"It needs lights," Autumn whispered.

"Camryn says we will shop tomorrow for decorations. We will buy these lights," Amme said. "And something called mistletoe."

"Blue ones," Autumn said.

"Her favorite color," Amme said, winking at Marcus.

"The same color as your swimsuit," Marcus said to Autumn, and he winked at Amme in return. "I'm all in favor of mistletoe, but we already have some. We'll put it up later."

"Ah! The same stuff Nanu mentioned earlier?" Amme asked.

"Yes."

Autumn gave him one of those shy smiles, and his own smile widened, emotion twisting his insides and leaving them in knots.

"Have you written your list for Santa Claus?" he asked.

Autumn fiddled with her hair, a trace of worry creasing her smooth brow. "No."

"Well." Marcus stood and held out his hand. "We need to get that sorted out and our list posted so Santa Claus knows to stop here at the farm. Back in a minute. We need paper and a pen."

"Who is this Santa Claus dude?" Nanu asked as Marcus led Autumn away to find paper.

Really? Marcus's brows rose as he walked inside. Who hadn't heard of Santa?

Later that night, after a fun dinner, Camryn declared she wanted to dance.

"Do you have any country music? I swear I haven't heard any for months," she said. "If you don't have country some good ole New Zealand tunes will work."

"That was a big yawn, sweetie. Time for you to go to bed." Amme stood and went to Autumn.

"Daddy, come too?" Autumn asked, sneaking a quick glance at him.

Marcus swallowed and managed a nod. "We need to discuss our plans for tomorrow."

"We're gonna email Santa," she whispered, her little girl lips curving in her shy smile, the one he was in love with. He followed Amme and Autumn up the stairs and to her bedroom.

"We're going with Camryn and the others to buy Christmas

decorations, and in the afternoon, we're all going to the beach," Amme said. "I think you'll enjoy that. I know I will."

"If you're wearing your bikini, I know I'll enjoy the view at the beach," Marcus said.

"Camryn said the beach is perfect for people-watching," Amme said. "We're going to play ball-volley."

Did she mean volleyball? Marcus wasn't sure, but he didn't try to correct her or ask questions. Instead, he enjoyed spending this time with his girls. The thought made him blink. His girls. When had that happened? This was only the second night and already he felt possessive.

"I have fun here, but I miss Mummy," Autumn said without warning.

Marcus glanced at Amme, the beginnings of panic stirring in him. Did she know how to handle this? Of course, the kid missed her mother, and she didn't know him well. This had to be weird for her.

"Did your mummy tell you she had to go away?" Amme asked.

Autumn nodded. "She was sick. She said she was tired, and she was sorry she wouldn't see me for a long time." She glanced at him, uncertainty in every line of her body. "How long?"

Amme sat on the bed and scooped Autumn up into her arms, holding her tight. "A long time, sweetheart. But did you know she can see you? She can see when you're happy or sad. She can see if you're behaving and eating your vegetables. She knows your swimming is improving."

"Really?"

"Yes," Amme said with such certainty that even Marcus decided to believe her. "I know she misses you, but she'll be spending time with people she knows there."

"Will they have cups of tea and biscuits?" Autumn asked.

"Yes," Amme said. "They have those scone things that Camryn talked about. Remember the ones she said she was going to teach us to make."

Autumn gave a thoughtful nod. "Mummy will have fun there. She knows how to make good cakes. She can show them how."

Amme pressed a kiss to the top of Autumn's head, and Marcus wondered if she did it to give herself a chance to rein in her galloping sympathy, to school her expression, to decide what to say to the little girl that might offer comfort. It was what he would have done because this situation was far, far, far away from his experience.

"Yes, she can teach them. I bet they'll have a lot of fun learning." Her voice held gravel, a distinct wobble, but she got the words out, and they seemed to comfort his daughter.

"Let's get you ready for bed. Your daddy can choose a book to read from while you clean your teeth and wash your face. The books we bought today are in the bag by the bed."

They disappeared, leaving Marcus bemused. Amme made Candy's death seem natural and not a bad thing. Her confident manner and the way she handled Autumn had stopped the tears before they started. He found the bag of books and picked out one featuring a naughty puppy that kept digging holes.

Amme helped Autumn into her pajamas and pulled back the covers. "Good night, sweetie." She kissed Autumn's cheek. "I'll plug in the special light we bought for you today while your father reads your story."

"What if the monsters come again?"

"Remember what Camryn said? That's a special light, and the monsters are frightened of it. I'm right next door, though, so if you need me for anything, just shout, and I'll come. Okay?"

Autumn's nod was solemn. "Yes."

Marcus started reading while Amme busied herself with unpacking the light. It was pale blue and the brim bore a sparkly unicorn. Subtle blue light lit the room when Amme switched it on.

"Pretty," she said. "Sweet dreams, Autumn."

"Where are you going?" Marcus asked.

"Downstairs to dance with my friends," Amme said.

"But what about me?"

"Autumn is almost asleep. You can handle finishing the story." With that said, she sashayed from the bedroom.

Marcus stared at her curvy ass and blinked when Autumn tugged at his arm.

"Keep reading, Daddy."

"Uh, okay." He scanned the page and started reading. "Bella, the white puppy, ran along the fence and searched for a way underneath." He kept turning pages until he reached the end, and his little girl had fallen asleep. He set the book down and backed out of the room, only pausing to switch off the main light.

As he approached the lounge, he started to hear music and laughter. He spied the mistletoe they'd hung from a light fitting and smiled. A country ballad drifted from his stereo system, and they were all dancing. Ry and Cameron were wrapped in each other's arms. Mogens was dancing with Gweneth, Jannike with Kaya and Amme partnered Nanu.

A spurt of jealousy swelled within Marcus.

"Good," Nanu said, grinning broadly when he spotted Marcus. "I need a rest. You can dance with Amme, and I'll take care of the music. Top system, Marcus. Rockin' music. Camryn was right, Amme. They have excellent music. We need to get some for the Indy. Ah...yeah. The music," Nanu said and backed away, a chagrined expression etched into his broad features.

"What is the Indy?" Marcus asked as he drew Amme closer.

"The name we give our vehicle."

The song drifted to an end. Nanu winked at him and put on another slow dance. Maybe his jealousy wasn't warranted. Marcus drew Amme even closer and ran his hand down her back.

"You smell nice," she whispered.

He grinned and brushed a kiss against her hair. She felt perfect in his arms.

"Did you buy anything else today, apart from the bikini?"

"Lingerie," she said with satisfaction. "I can't wait to show you."

"So you mean to entice me?" Laughter shaded his voice while a whoosh of blood settled in his cock.

"Of course I do," she said, her face devoid of humor. "Is it working?"

Marcus stared. As a businessman, he was used to reading people, making snap decisions, yet Amme... He found himself shaking his head. "I have trouble knowing if you're joking or not."

"I'm not joking. I find you attractive. Camryn says normally, an employee shouldn't make advances to their boss, but since we're leaving at the beginning of the year, it would be all right. As long as you are interested in return."

Marcus found himself charmed and incredibly turned on. He cupped her cheek and tipped up her chin until their gazes meshed. Her skin was cool and soft beneath his fingertips. "I'm interested."

"Perfect. What do we do next?"

A laugh spluttered from him, loud enough to attract the attention of her friends. He gave her a swift hug, reveling in her softness against his harder body.

Behind him someone spoke in staccato clicks and grunts.

"What is that language?" he asked.

"Jibberish," Amme said. "They're being silly. Private joke."

"As long as they're not making fun about my big ears or pointy nose."

"No, they're giving me advice and made mention of your sexy arse."

Marcus spluttered another laugh and brushed a kiss on her cheek. Refreshing. That was the word for Amme. She was light years away from the women he normally associated with—their coy games and manipulations. A few weeks in her company was just the thing he needed to recharge. Amme was the perfect prescription for both him and Autumn.

"You're standing under the mistletoe," Nanu said without warning.

Marcus glanced up. Nope. It wasn't him. His gaze went to Amme's lips and lingered. Pity. Maybe he'd maneuver Amme in that direction.

Shrill whistles and cheers dragged him back. He turned to see Kaya plant a big, wet kiss on Jannike. Jannike's arms went around the other woman and she kissed her back. Camryn started giggling, laughing so hard Ry had to hold her upright.

"Woot. Woot. *Woot!*" Nanu cried.

Gweneth clapped her hands together, her pretty face beaming.

"Are they together?" Marcus asked.

"What? We're all together," Amme said.

As his mind groped with that, the music changed to something older and more upbeat.

"Do you know how to do this one?" Amme asked. "I saw it on the television."

"I'm sure I can muddle through," Marcus said and began the steps to the jive. Amme studied him for a few seconds then fell into step, looking as if she'd been doing the dance for years. "You're good."

"Show us the steps," Kaya said from behind them.

Marcus turned Amme a fraction but continued to dance. Kaya watched closely and started to follow with Jannike as her partner. Her hair looked bluer tonight. It wasn't unattractive, just bright. Was that—her ear was pointy and decorated with some sort of jewelry. He blinked and looked again, but her hair had flipped over her ear.

"Something wrong?" Amme asked when the dance brought them closer.

He glanced over her shoulder and felt his eyes widen on seeing

Mogens. The man glowed with a weird pearly light.

"No. I guess I'm tired." He must be if he was seeing things. Marcus risked another glance, and both Mogens and Kaya appeared normal again.

The music drifted to an end.

"Someone is under the mistletoe," Nanu said.

Good. He'd got it right this time. Marcus turned to Amme and started to move toward her. A big blur passed between them, and before he could blink, hard hands seized him, and a mouth marauded his. Shock held him in place. There were cheers. Whistles. Someone laughed so hard they were having trouble breathing.

"Hey," Nanu said, drawing back with a scowl. "You're meant to kiss me back."

Camryn gasped a hoarse breath and started laughing again. Tears streamed from her eyes.

"Why didn't you kiss me back?" Nanu demanded. "Those are the mistletoe rules."

Camryn drew a noisy breath. Her mouth twitched, and she let out another big howl of laughter.

"I...ah...I don't swing that way," Marcus finally managed.

"Why is she laughing?" Jannike demanded.

Everyone was looking puzzled, apart from Camryn, and she was no help because she couldn't stop hooting.

"Traditionally, kissing under the mistletoe occurs between men and women," Marcus said, edging away from Nanu. He wrapped his arm around Amme's waist then moved her in front of him so Nanu couldn't pounce on him again. "A young woman would stand under the mistletoe on purpose in order to get a man she liked to kiss her. These days, with same-sex marriages, I presume women kiss each other too. And men kiss each other. You're not meant to kiss just anyone," Marcus said. "Normally, you're showing you like them."

SHELLEY MUNRO

"I do like you," Nanu said, his broad forehead a mass of wrinkles.

Camryn, who'd eased off her laughing, started chortling again.

"But you don't want to have sex with me, right?" Marcus steeled himself for the answer.

"No, I don't want to fukk you," Nanu said. "I wouldn't try to steal you from Amme. Friends don't do that."

"Nanu!" Camryn shrieked and burst into giggles.

Kaya glowered at Camryn. "You lied to us."

"D-didn't."

"But you didn't explain properly," Amme said, the corners of her eyes crinkling.

"Payback!" Camryn shouted in triumph. "Marcus, is Nanu a good kisser?"

"I was too shocked to notice," he said.

"I'm an excellent kisser," Nanu said. "I could kiss you again."

"No," Marcus said and drew Amme against his chest. "We're good."

Camryn showed signs of succumbing again. Nanu snorted. "More music."

"No, Marcus is tired," Amme said. "All the physical work today has tired him out. You need to go home now. I don't want him exhausted."

"He needs to recover from Nanu's kiss," Camryn said.

Marcus spluttered, especially when Camryn winked at him. He willed the heat from his cheeks and only partially succeeded.

"We'll go," Ry said. "You'll probably see a lot of us because Amme and the others are here. Feel free to tell us to leave."

"I'm tired too," Camryn said. "We have a full day planned tomorrow. I might ask Max if Luke can come to the beach with us. He'll be company for Autumn."

"Satisfactory plan," Amme said. "See you tomorrow."

Marcus stood at Amme's side and waved goodbye to her friends.

66

"Thank you for letting us use your cottage," Amme said.

"You're doing me a favor. I think I'm getting the best deal."

"You are paying me," Amme reminded him, and just like that, some of his feel-good mood dissipated.

Doubt demons lunged, their clawed hands grabbing him by the neck. Him—the man who radiated confidence. He hesitated to voice them, then decided to follow Amme's example and forget the filters. "Is that why you're propositioning me? Because I'm paying you?"

"My employment looking after Autumn is separate. I am a child minder. Sex is not my job."

"Oh." The way she expressed herself seemed strange. "So if I was to try to kiss you now, you'd let me because you want a kiss, not because I'm your employer."

"I wanted your kiss from the first sec I saw you." Her whiskey eyes simmered with truth and sincerity, and he believed every word. "Kissing you, touching you is not part of my job description."

"Excellent." Marcus led her back inside and came to a halt in the kitchen. "The dishes are done."

"My friends would have done them," Amme said.

"I think I'll keep them around. My friends would never think of cleaning up after dinner."

Amme wove their fingers together. "Maybe you need new friends."

He tugged her closer, his pulse rate high jumping as he studied her. Her features were neat and perfect and her skin didn't bear a single blemish. Amme was stunning, and he couldn't wait to run his hands over the curves he'd seen on display when she wore her bikini.

Her eyes widened as he backed her against the kitchen counter. Once she was trapped, he cupped her jaw with both hands and leaned in to kiss her. Her lips were cold but they moved under his and parted when he traced the seam with the tip of his tongue. Sweet. She tasted of wine and a hint of chocolate. When she let out a tiny groan and softened, he took the kiss deeper and buried his fingers in her hair, plundering her mouth and enjoying the hell out of the act. Long moments later, he lifted his head and grinned when she breathed hard. He rubbed his nose against hers then kissed her again, using every bit of his skill, his hands skimming down to settle on her hips.

He notched his cock against her softness and rocked, his blood pounding hotly through his veins. Damn. He'd spent a weekend with an old friend a couple of weeks ago and the sex had been hot and fulfilling. But something about this woman took his desire to another level. He wanted her in his bed. He wanted her naked. He wanted her now.

Amme was sure her main processing unit flew offline when Marcus started kissing her. Her brain ceased to process the separate emotions and sensations, and she wallowed in the pleasure of his touch, hanging on to his shoulders for purchase. Luckily, the rigid counter at her back helped prop her upright, otherwise she feared she'd end in a wet puddle at his feet.

He lifted his mouth, parting their lips, and she saw his brown gaze appeared lighter than usual, almost amber. Pretty.

"Come to my bedroom," he whispered.

Never had words sounded so sweet and enticing. She found herself nodding, her processing unit still sluggish. He twined his fingers with hers and tugged her from the kitchen. He switched off lights as they made their way to the stairs, and she tried to input information into her brain. It didn't stick. She'd ask Camryn tomorrow if this was normal with human sex. Her brain had never hiccupped in this manner before.

"I should check on Autumn," Amme said. At least her main processing unit wasn't switching off this part of her—the purpose for which she was conceived and her enhancements prioritized.

"We'll both do it," Marcus whispered.

She watched him as he studied his daughter, able to discern his baffled yet tender expression in the dim light. The appearance of a daughter might have shocked him, but he appeared determined to do his best. The knowledge warmed her through and made her like him even more.

"She is in a deep sleep. I doubt she will awaken tonight," Amme said.

"How do you know?"

"I have a lot of experience with children," Amme whispered. "Besides, even if she does prove me wrong, we will hear her."

"I bow to your experience."

"I don't require that," Amme said.

Marcus chuckled and caressed her cheek. "I enjoy your quaint expressions."

Amme frowned inside. Was this good or bad? The last thing she wanted was to put herself or her friends in danger. Nanu had slipped with his English tonight. No doubt Ry would remind him not to lapse again.

"My bedroom," he reminded her.

"Wait. I want to try out my lingerie," Amme said.

"Aren't you wearing it?"

"Some," Amme said. "But I have special night lingerie."

"Tomorrow," Marcus said as he hustled her past her bedroom door. "I'm too impatient."

"Oh." The pressure of his hand at the small of her back reinforced his words, and she let him guide her into his bedroom. He shut the door behind them and switched on a light.

The room smelled of him—musky with sweet and spicy undertones—and she hummed a note of pleasure.

"I want you naked," he said, and he prowled toward her in the same manner Ry stalked Camryn.

"Yes." It was all she could say as she attempted to fight the weird tingles bombarding her person. Her main processor was hiccupping again, reducing her ability to multitask.

"Sit on the edge of the bed."

An order she gladly followed.

He unfastened her sandals and tossed each one aside.

"You can stand again."

Amme stood, and he straightened from his crouch.

"Turn around."

She presented her back and felt his cool hands at the fastening of her sundress. The zipper rasped as he tugged it down, and the material fell away from her breasts. Marcus gave an audible swallow, and she grinned—a private one of triumph and success. Her plan was working. Kaya would seethe with jealousy—if she could tear her mind off the chocolate substance. Another sound emerged from him—a soft groan—focusing Amme. His hands trembled before he guided the material down her body and over her hips.

He cleared his throat. "Turn around."

She obeyed, eager to see his reaction. Her lingerie was black lace and concealed and revealed at the same time. Not much more substantial than a promise, Camryn had said.

"Beautiful." He dragged a single finger over the swell of one breast, leaving a tickling sensation in his wake. He repeated the move, but in the opposite direction, and this time, she shivered.

"That feels very nice. A touch doesn't normally do that to me."

He paused to shoot her a look. "No interruptions." His tone was terse, and she frowned.

"Are you angry with me?"

"I don't like to think about other men touching you."

"It's not the same," she said, fumbling for words to make him understand. "It...they didn't make me shiver."

He smiled suddenly, a bright ray of sunshine that allowed her to relax. "Good to know." He slipped a finger beneath the shoulder strap and gave a slight tug. "This is too pretty to rip, but I want you naked so bad."

"Yes," she agreed. "You could go much faster."

He caught her gaze, and her tummy did a funny shimmy as if tiny nanobugs were doing a jitterbug dance inside her body. She couldn't look away from his pretty eyes. They were magnetic and compelled her to do...something. She wasn't sure what.

"Faster isn't always good. Not if I want to make memories."

"Oh." He said the most perfect things. That was her wish—memories to sustain her during the long space voyage to Viros. Although they'd make provisioning stops and intended to make a return visit to Kaya's brother on Slyvia, travel through space ticked over in long and wearisome rotations.

"Hey!" He clicked his fingers way too close to her nose. "I'm here. Where did you go?"

"Racing onward," she murmured. "Thinking about how you'll feel plunging deep into my quim."

"Your what?"

Oops. Different term on Earth. She shot him a saucy wink. "My pussy."

His pupils darkened secs before he lifted and tossed her on his bed. Before her receptors registered and reported to her brain, he caged her on the mattress, his broad shoulders and the muscles of his arms flexing as he rose over her.

She blinked up at him. "My, what big muscles you have."

"Impudent baggage." Shaking his head, he used his mouth to follow the same path his finger had traveled earlier.

Another one of those shivers slipped through her muscles, her sensors telegraphing loud and excited enjoyment even as she wondered about the definition of a baggage. Amme shoved the puzzlement away for later. This Earthman held great promise, and she didn't want to miss a thing.

"A front-fastening bra," he said. "How convenient."

"How did you know?" She hadn't seen one before today.

He hesitated. "I've seen this style before."

"Oh." Well, now she knew how it felt to hear about other lovers. Not pleasant. "I don't wish to hear of other lovers either."

"Deal. Let's shove them out of this bed." He deftly flicked the fastening, and it opened to free her breasts.

"Yes." The word came out in a hiss, since he was busy exploring one breast with his tongue. The nearer his mouth moved to the tip of her breast, the faster her heart-pump raced. Her secondary heart—well, it was galloping—and for a sec, she weighed up asking him to stop. The last thing she wanted was an explosion due to a faulty heart-pump.

But he closed his mouth around the tip of her breast and drew hard, driving her mind back to sexual enjoyment. A ribbon of sensation slid along her bloodlines to converge at her sexual center. Her hands, unguided by her central system, slid into his brown hair and tugged, exerting force when he indicated he might stop this miraculous pleasure.

"Shush, sweetheart. I'm not going to stop. I want to take off your bra so it won't be in the way."

She pushed out a breath and released the life grip she had on his skull. "Okay."

He helped her sit and deftly slid her bra down her arms then tossed it aside. "We'll take these pretty panties off at the same time." As he spoke, he drew them down her legs, and her panties joined her bra on the floor.

A knife of tension struck her then, as she waited for his reaction. Her mons was bare. Oh, she had the right explanation for the lack of pubic hair, but Marcus didn't bother to ask a single question. He stared, taking her in, and a slow smile curled across his lips.

"Gorgeous," he whispered, his gaze glowing with golden lights. She basked under his appreciation, shivered when he ran his fingers down her torso from breast to hip. At least she had a belly button. Jannike and Kaya didn't because they were grown in birth labs. Mogens had designed a patch for them to wear so the humans didn't notice when they wore bikinis or got naked.

"Part your legs for me, sweetheart." The husky sound of his voice stroked across her receptors, bringing another wash of enjoyment.

She followed his instruction and parted her legs.

"Yeah, just like that. Don't move a muscle."

He positioned his body in the gap between the V of her legs and studied her so intently she wondered if he'd noticed something out of the ordinary. Camryn had said their bodies were similar, but the tension yanked at her, and Amme bit her lip. She'd be mortified if he pulled away in rejection.

Finally, finally, he lifted his head and meshed their gazes. "You are perfect. I don't know where to touch first."

"Everywhere," she instructed.

Marcus chuckled, the infectious sound tugging at her lips as he leaned over to kiss her. His lips were firm, and his tongue forceful as he stroked into her mouth. After devouring her and stamping her with his taste and scent, he kissed a trail across her jaw and down her neck. He licked her collarbone—a warm wash of wet heat—and as he moved lower, her heart-pump did a crazy jig. She moaned, struggling to keep up with the lusty messages bombarding her brain. She writhed and arched her body, silently pleading with him to touch her breasts.

"Steady, sweetheart. We have plenty of time."

"Marcus." His name was a protest.

He removed his lips from the curve of her breast and lifted his gaze. "Amme." Humor painted his features, making him appear years younger and so, so tempting. "I love the way you say my name."

"Marcus." She inhaled sharply and fought to contain the raw need bombarding her tronics. This—being with Marcus—was different from her experience with other males. "Please touch me. Please, Marcus. Please."

"With pleasure," he whispered, and he took one nipple into his mouth, flicking and teasing the tender peak with his tongue while his hands wandered lower. Warm palms slid along the sensitive skin of her inner thighs then drifted higher to press his fingers against her core. A jolt zapped her and a rough gasp squeezed up her throat.

"More," she whispered.

"Demanding thing, aren't you?"

"I know what I want. I want you."

"Soon." He sparkled with devilment, something she hadn't seen in him before, and it charmed her, made her smile in return. He moved farther down the bed and kissed her inner thigh. The stubble on his cheek provided decadent friction and dragged another gasp from deep in her throat.

"Marcus."

He laughed, a warm puff of air against her folds. Her hips jerked upward and pushed her against his mouth.

"Marcus. That...ah..." She held him in place, or at least attempted to. He chuckled, the sound a blast of sensation against her sensitive flesh. His tongue circled her sex pulse—no, her clitoris or that was what Camryn said it was called—electrifying her receptors and shooting a lusty message to her brain. She rocked against him, greedily wanting more, more, more of his touch.

The shock of his fingers pumping inside her was a pleasant one, the deliberate curl of his digits hitting a happy spot deep inside that made her jolt and heavy breathe.

Oh, that was excellent and so much better than her recollections promised. He pumped his fingers inside her again, and she felt a surge of wetness, her body preparing her for his possession.

"Marcus." His name was a plea for him to do something, and finally, he did. His mouth closed over her clitoris while his fingers stroked her internally. The push and drag stimulated inner nerves on the way in and massaged them in a delightful manner on the way out. The hot pleasure grew bigger and swelled until she wondered if her body could contain the sweet bliss. She gasped, she groaned, her receptors vibrating, trembling on the cusp of something splendid. The next stroke of his tongue shoved the great into an explosion of acute, almost painful pleasure. She cried out, so ruffled and out of control she thought she might be speaking Universal instead of Earth speak. Aware of the danger, she bit her lip, the nip of pain grounding her, balancing the wicked, wicked bliss tossing her receptors into chaos.

Marcus licked her, a gentle flick of warmth, and another spasm poured along her lifeblood network. Gradually, the sensations trailed off to leave inner contentment. He pulled back and rose up her body. Too comfortable to speak, she merely moaned her protest. A nip at her breast made her jump, her eyes snap open in confusion.

"God, you're beautiful," he murmured. "I haven't been able to think of anything except fucking your sexy body since the moment I first saw you."

He kissed her, a gentle, sweet exchange that stole her breath along with the remnants of her sanity. Her heart-pump went boom-boom-boom, the sound so loud Amme wondered if Marcus would hear the racket.

Distraction. "Are you going to take off your clothes soon?"

"You bet." He stood and unbuttoned his shirt, one small white button at a time. Slowly the edges of his garment parted to reveal hard tanned muscles. Without taking his gaze off her, he tugged the shirt down his arms and let it drift to the floor.

She pillowed her hands and made no secret of her interest. "I like looking at you."

"Same goes."

"You should keep undressing."

"I can do that." His gaze remained on her as his hands went to the button on his jeans. She watched them slide down his muscular legs. His black underwear went next, and her attention settled on his cock. The working part looked the same as others she'd experienced. She chewed on her bottom lip. Apart from the tentacles, of course, because Jannike and Kaya agreed. Tentacle sex was in a class of its own.

He reached over and opened a drawer. The foil packet he pulled out and opened must be one of the condoms Camryn had mentioned during a sex talk. Curious, she watched him roll it up his male part. He didn't need to use this, but she couldn't tell him without inviting questions.

"I can't wait to fuck you," he said, his features full of cheeky attitude again, yet there was hunger and desire too, and her insides quaked in anticipation.

"Fuck is such a raw word."

His brows rose, and his lips lifted at the corners in a half-grin. "You don't approve?"

"Undecided," she said. "No, not true. I have no opinion at present, but I do want to have sex with you."

"That's a relief." He stretched out beside her. Instead of sticking his cock straight inside her, he started to kiss her again. Slow, easy kisses that made her want to moan aloud. He was gentle with her when other men had become aggressive and handled her roughly, simply because they knew she was robust. A peculiar tingling started in the region of her eyes. She cataloged the anomaly and continued to return the caresses of Marcus's lips. Their tongues tangled, and another wave of sensations writhed through her circuits and lifeblood network.

Already, she wanted to have another one of those toe-curling explosions. Probably plain greedy. "I like kissing you." The words leaped from her mouth without warning, sudden and unexpected before her tronics had approved the sentiment.

"I like everything about you, Amme." He thrust inside her with one hard stroke of his cock.

Every nerve in her...pussy stood and saluted. Such a silly word, but Camryn—Marcus pulled back and filled her again. Every substantial thought faded into mist. She squeezed her lips together to hold back her groan, but a satisfied keen escaped anyway. He felt big and strong and so right plunging into her body, stirring her inner receptors with his thrust-and-retreat motions.

"This is good too."

He barked out a laugh. "We'd have a problem if you didn't like it. You're so tight, sweetheart. Your pussy feels snug and warm. Perfect."

She was designed to give the perfect fit to each male. Not that she could tell Marcus. He seemed decent, but some males loathed machines or any of her race who were part machine. She'd learned this to her cost and never willingly shared the information.

He withdrew and thrust into her heat again, his forceful stroke wringing a groan from her throat.

Marcus stilled, embedded deep inside her. "Did I hurt you?" Strain throbbed in his voice and a tremor worked through his muscular arms.

"I don't mind sex a little rough. I'm not a weakling."

"No you're not." His gorgeous grin lit up his harsh features. "Hold tight now."

Marcus set up a fast invade and retreat, and Amme clung. His musky scent deepened as did her own. Pleasure swirled just out of reach, but she didn't complain. Instead she enjoyed his touch, the way he imprinted his scent on her, his touch. She recorded every detail for later memories.

"Kiss me," he ground out and slipped a hand between their bodies to rub back and forth over her sex center.

Barely able to grasp his words, she dallied, luxuriating in the swirl of pleasure that surged forth with every stroke of his fingers.

"Kiss me." She complied in a daze, the kiss slow and sensual and holding a different flavor. Passionate and eager, all-encompassing. He devoured her mouth as he plunged into her with extra hard strokes. On the third thrust, he stopped, and a masculine growl escaped with his next kiss. Against her chest, she could feel the pump of his heart, and deep inside her body, she registered the spurt of his seed.

"Amme." His clever fingers whisked across her sex center in the perfect manner.

She jolted and climaxed in a hard series of pulses that flared bright colors across her closed eyelids. "Marcus." His name was a whisper of contentment.

"That was incredible. I haven't...I don't... It's never been like that before."

"For me either," she said.

Their next kiss was gentle and soft. Tender. For Amme, it said everything she couldn't tell him. She liked him very, very much but come the beginning of the year, she'd depart with her friends.

The idea of leaving Marcus made her heart-pump stutter.

"Sleep with me tonight?"

"Yes, please." Another new experience. Ry and Camryn always shared a bed, and she'd wondered if the intimacy would become obtrusive and annoying. Here was a chance to discover the answer to her intrigue.

Marcus pulled from her body and levered away. Curious, she watched him remove and discard the condom. He was back in secs and slid into the bed. After switching off the light, his arms slid around her, his breath warm against her neck.

"Thank you, Marcus. I enjoyed that very much."

"You say that like it was a once-off." It wasn't difficult to hear his frown. "I want you again, have you sleep in my bed every night."

"Yes." That word made her belly roil and her senses leap. "Yes."

"Perfect." A kiss landed on her cheek. "Because that's what I want too."

Very good, Amme thought, and she sent her systems into rest mode, a smile of happiness curving her lips.

CHAPTER FIVE

"That was a fun night," Camryn said.

Ry opened the door and urged her inside her cottage. "It was. Marcus seems like a decent man."

"He's not stupid. Nanu slipped a couple of times. He needs to remember his English because we don't want to attract attention."

A tap sounded on the door Ry had just closed. Camryn scented the new arrival, the quick rise of tension fading into welcome.

"It's Max." She opened the door and grinned at her twin. "I missed you so much. It's gonna be hard to leave, although Ry says we can come and visit again."

Her twin's smile faltered, and her feline senses picked up the strain in his body, his discomfort.

"What is it? What's wrong?" she asked.

"Come in," Ry said.

Max dithered on the doorstep then sighed, his shoulders

drooping into a pose resembling misery. He cleared his throat, shot them an apologetic look. "Ellen said if I don't return to the house in half an hour, she'll call the authorities." He focused on Ry. "She's worried you're going to attack me. She's already forbidden Luke to come anywhere near either of you."

"I'm sorry." Melancholy popped like an overfull balloon inside her, tensing her muscles and stirring her feline into a grumbling frenzy. She batted her feline down and forced her uncooperative mouth to produce and understanding smile. A visit. Was that too much to ask? "The last thing I want is to cause trouble between you and Ellen. But you should know I can shift into a feline. It's not just Ry."

Max's mouth dropped open, and he didn't shut it again until Camryn reached over to push his jaw into the closed position. He studied her like he scrutinized the horses he trained, but in this case, his watchfulness suggested he was waiting for her to chuckle—to let him in on the joke.

When she remained silent, watchful, he broke first. "You're kidding."

"Nope. I can prove it if you want."

"Fuck," Max said, his posture one of uncertainty, of a man waiting for the knife to fall. "I'm not sure whether to believe you or not."

"Believe it." Camryn flexed her shoulders and sent calming thoughts to her agitated feline. The wild part of her wanted to drum sense into her twin. The human part knew the importance of communication. "It came as a shock to me too. Not that I regret a moment. Ry and his crew kidnapping me was a turning point. They saved me from wrecking my life. Ry gave me purpose."

"She fought us, or rather me, every minute of the way," Ry said.

Max's brows drew together in a visual question mark. "You really came for me?"

"Yes." Ry confirmed his words with a nod, matter-of-fact and unrepentant. "As it happened, we made the best choice. No offense."

"None taken," Max said, but his frown deepened, discomfort broadcasting like a communication satellite.

"What is it, Max?" Camryn asked.

"I promised Ellen I'd take her and Luke to spend Christmas week with her family in Taupo. I want to spend time with you but…" He trailed off, a man unhappy with his message yet stuck between the love for his wife and his twin.

"Ellen doesn't approve of me." Camryn tried to pretend it didn't hurt. She didn't fool Ry, and he was at her side in secs flat, his muscular presence the strength to lend her courage.

"She doesn't believe you've changed, and she's terrified one of your friends will hurt us," Max said with a grimace.

"That will only happen if you physically attack Camryn," Ry said. "It's easy to see you love her, so you're safe."

"Ellen is worried about Marcus and his little girl. She wavers between telling them the truth and reporting you to the authorities."

"No!" Camryn planted herself in front of her brother. "Max, you can't let her do that. No one will believe her. Hell, they'd probably ship her off for a psych evaluation. They might even decide she's not stable enough to keep her babies. Has she considered that? Amme was designed for childcare. The children of her planet are scanned at birth and their natural inclinations are enhanced with cybertronics to make them exceptional at their jobs. You couldn't find a better nanny. She'd put her life in danger rather than let Autumn injure herself. I promise both of them are safe. You must make Ellen understand."

"I've tried and tried to think of an alternative, but I've decided it would be best if I take Ellen and Luke to Taupo as we'd planned," Max said, glancing once at his twin, then allowing his gaze to shoot to his balled fingers. "It will give Ellen the distance to gain perspective. When are you going to leave?"

"The second or third of January. It's a long journey to Viros," Ry said.

"All right. How about this?" Max asked. "I'll make sure we're back here between Christmas and the New Year. We'll have a party to celebrate the New Year. At least by then Ellen should be more confident you're not here to start an alien invasion."

Camryn scowled. "I don't like it, but I won't cause trouble. We're going to the beach tomorrow afternoon. Would you and Ellen and Luke like to come? Who is looking after the farm while you're gone? You have horses in training."

"I have a couple of employees who live in the Karaka area. I was going to ask them. I don't suppose you'd be willing to help out."

"We'd be happy to aid you," Ry said.

"I'd love to," Camryn said at the same time. "Although the horses might sense my feline self. That might be a problem."

Max blinked. "You're serious, aren't you?"

"Yes," Camryn said.

"Okay. I'll talk to Ellen about the beach. She probably won't want to come, because she's busy with Christmas baking, but Luke and I will go with you. I'll persuade her somehow."

"I've missed you, Max." Camryn wrapped her arms around her brother, clung for a luxurious moment, and wallowed in the scent of family.

"Likewise," Max said. "You really came here on a spaceship?"

Camryn rolled her eyes. "Last time I looked, I didn't have wings."

"We'll give you a tour if you want," Ry said. "We need to do some repairs and maintenance before we leave."

"Deal!" Max checked his watch. "My half an hour is up. I'd better get back to Ellen. You coming down to the stables tomorrow morning?"

"Yes," Camryn said and kissed her brother on the cheek. "See you tomorrow."

"You're disappointed," Ry said once Max left.

"A little. I would have liked to share Christmas Day with my brother and keep up the traditions our parents started. It's silly, I know."

"It's not silly. We'll make our day special and start our own traditions. We can continue them wherever we find ourselves on Christmas Day."

"I love you, Ry," she said, her heart aching with the hugeness of her emotions.

"Love you too, kitten." He took her hand and led her toward the bedroom. "Let me prove it."

"Excellent idea," she said with a saucy wink and a hip bump. "You need to keep reminding me, or I might think I dreamed the entire alien experience." She let out a shriek when he pinched her bottom and growled.

"You'd better run, little girl," he said, his voice full of feline.

Camryn took one look at her mate, ripped her hand free, and ran right into the bedroom.

"I haven't been to the beach before," Amme said.

"No?" Marcus shot a puzzled glance at her, and she realized she'd erred with her throwaway comment. He pulled into the driveway of Max's farm and stopped outside their door. "Wait there. I'll go and tell Max we're here."

Before he could climb from his vehicle, the front door opened, and Luke ran out carrying a ball and a towel.

Amme grinned at the little boy. "Someone is excited."

"I want to swim," Autumn said from her car seat.

"We're all going to swim," Marcus said, sharing a grin with

Amme.

The bright smile turned her insides rebellious. They swooped and dived and didn't behave in the correct cyborg manner. This wasn't the time for a malfunction, yet she couldn't help but enjoy his sparkling happiness. Amme gave a soft sigh as he went to help Max with the car seat for Luke. Marcus had made this holiday feel special—a celebration of home. In a short time she'd become attached to Autumn, which was the way her programming should work, but this tie to Marcus...

The rear door opened, and Max deftly fixed Luke's car seat in place. In a matter of mins, he had his son buckled in and ready to depart.

"Is Ellen coming with us?" Marcus asked.

Max shot a quick apologetic glance to Amme. "No, she has a lot of Christmas baking to do. She's making edible gifts for her sisters and cooking a Christmas cake to take with us to Taupo."

"Oh," Amme said. "I thought...Camryn said we would have Christmas dinner here. She must be disappointed. I know she was looking forward to it."

Max's expression wiped clean, yet Amme sensed his tension and anguish at the strain between his wife and his twin sister.

"We can have Christmas dinner at my place," Marcus said as he pulled out of the driveway. "Still plenty of time to arrange it, and we already have our trees."

Max shrugged, and Amme picked up another wave of his unhappiness. "I'd promised Ellen already, and I don't want to disappoint her. I suggested to Camryn we have a party to celebrate the new year instead."

"Good idea," Marcus said. "Since you'll be away, why don't we have it at my place? I have plenty of helpers." He winked at Amme. "Your friends seem to relish organizing things."

"That's a fine plan," Amme said. "That way, Ellen won't have to race home and organize a party."

"We'll invite the neighbors and some of my friends," Marcus said. "How does that sound?"

Max shared another quick look with Amme, or at least their gazes connected when she glanced back. "That would work. It's a great idea, and I know it'd reassure Ellen. She's stressed at the moment, and it's not good for the babies."

The babies might be a factor, but Amme knew Ellen didn't want her house overrun with aliens. At least Camryn's brother seemed more open-minded.

"What is the name of this beach?" Amme asked. "Camryn calls it Ma Right Eye. That can't be right?"

Max burst out laughing. "You mean Maraetai. It's ma-rye-a-tie. The Māori language can confuse visitors."

"One day, not long ago, she had us laughing until we were crying when she was explaining some of the names. Some of them sound rude to foreigners." She glanced at the kids, saw they were chattering together. "Why-poo?"

Max barked out a laugh. "You mean Waipu. Trust Camryn."

Conversation flowed after that, ranging from Christmas to horses to business and beaches. The drive took them through the outskirts of a town and into the countryside. After the nothingness of space, the lush green pastures dotted with trees and grazing animals were a visual feast.

"There are lots of different animals," Amme said, frowning at one they passed. It was small, white, and shaggy, with horns curling from its head. She had no idea what classification the creature fell into but didn't like to ask too many questions in front of Marcus.

"This is perfect farming country," Marcus said. "You find alpacas, cattle, and sheep along with some stud horse farms. Some farmers grow crops."

Amme nodded and kept watching the landscape.

"Are you going to the Christmas parade?" Max asked.

"I hadn't thought about it," Marcus said.

"We were going to take Luke. He wants to see Santa Claus arrive on the fire engine," Max said.

"I want to go." Amme had discussed the Santa Claus dude with the others, and Camryn had shown them pictures. Now she wanted to see the phenomenon in person. "I'll take Autumn."

"When is it?" Marcus asked.

"This coming Saturday," Max said.

"Sounds doable. I'll mark it in my calendar."

"Ooh. The sea," Amme said on catching a glimpse of water.

"Where?" Luke demanded.

Autumn remained silent but craned her neck, struggling to see out the window.

Marcus chuckled. "I can't decide who is the biggest kid."

Amme pulled a face. Too bad. She couldn't tell him these experiences were brand, shiny new. Her jobs had confined her to cities, mostly big ones with not a trace of plant material. Earth, with its gorgeous scenery and lack of technology, thrilled her.

"What are those trees with the red flowers?" The trees clung to cliffs and banks all along the coast road, the scarlet red of the flowers drawing her eye.

"Those are pohutukawa trees," Marcus said. "They flower during December, and they've become a symbol of a New Zealand Christmas."

"Pretty," Amme said. "I should've brought a..." She frowned while trying to remember the correct word.

"I have a camera," Max said. "We'll take some group photos if you want. You'll see more pohutukawa trees at the beach. I can email the photos to Camryn."

"Yes, camera. Thank you. There's the van," Amme said. "Will the water be cold?"

"Maybe at first." Marcus parked beside the black van and pulled out his phone. He keyed in something and winked at Autumn. "There, now we won't forget the Christmas parade." As he placed the phone back in his pocket, it buzzed. He glanced at the screen, scowled, and shoved his phone under the car seat out of sight. "Who wants a swim?"

"Me, me!" Luke jumped up and down and reminded Amme of Camryn.

"He reminds me of Camryn," she said and took Autumn's hand to stop her tearing after Luke.

"Swim," Autumn said.

"As soon as we get organized," Marcus said.

"How long?" Autumn asked, her delicate brows puckering.

"We need to stake our place on the beach first," Marcus said.

"Suntan lotion first," Max said to his excited son once they'd settled in a flurry of rainbow-colored beach towels, buckets and spades, picnic baskets and a red-and-white umbrella. "Put on your hat."

"What is the purpose of the lotion?" Amme said in an undertone to Camryn. "Should I have some for Autumn?"

"Yes. Max won't mind sharing. Humans need it to stop the sun burning their skin," Camryn whispered. "That's the reason for the hat too."

"We don't have a hat for Autumn," Amme said to Marcus. "We don't want her face to burn."

"Good point," Marcus said. "From memory, there's a shop just down the road. They'll sell hats."

"I want to swim," Kaya said.

"You're all as bad as each other," Max said. "Don't you have beaches where you live?"

"No," Jannike said. "I've never seen the sea before."

"Okay," said Camryn, and she started flinging off her clothes to reveal her red bikini. "Last one in is a rotten egg."

Ry let out a kitty purr and yanked his T-shirt over his head. He chased after his mate with another rumble that made Camryn screech out a laugh.

"They growl a lot," Max said, grinning after his sister.

"It's a feline thing," Amme said without thinking.

"A feline thing?" Marcus asked.

"Family joke," Max said smoothly before he turned away to supervise Luke.

Marcus cast a quick glance at Amme, who was chewing her bottom lip. A sign of guilt? But guilt about what? She had clearly said feline, which was plain weird. Lots of things didn't add up when it came to Amme and her friends. Their odd expressions and the way everything seemed new to them. His gaze cut to Max as he pondered the facts he'd gathered. Nah, nothing to worry about. Amme was fantastic with Autumn. Hell, he liked her too and didn't want his nosy questions to upset their current situation.

Amme dumped her bag and two beach towels onto the shell-strewn beach. She crouched beside Autumn and helped her strip down to her swimsuit.

Amme glanced up at him and smiled. Something twisted inside his chest, pulled tight until he had to concentrate on breathing. Last night with Amme...the sex had been amazing and the lazy loving this morning was the perfect way to start a day.

"Are you just gonna stare?" she asked.

"I like looking at my girls." The words slipped out naturally—words he'd never thought he'd hear himself utter.

"Your girls are going swimming," Amme said. "Right, Autumn?"

His daughter nodded.

"Swim. Swim," Luke chanted.

Marcus took off his T-shirt and reached for Autumn's hand. "Ready?"

"I want Amme," she said.

"Just a sec," Amme said, and she stripped off her T-shirt and shorts with economical movements to reveal a bronze-colored bikini.

"I want Amme too," Marcus said in a low voice, which only she could hear.

She tossed him a grin and took Autumn's other hand.

The rest of Amme's friends were already in the water, shouting and splashing as if they'd never swum in the sea before. Their behavior raised those questions again. He cast a glance at Max, who was shaking his head at their antics. He didn't seem surprised. Maybe he'd ask Max a few questions when he could speak to him in private.

He and Amme walked to the water's edge at Autumn's pace. They lifted her over a small wave, and she shrieked. Marcus chuckled and stepped into deeper water until Autumn was up to her waist. His happy mood took a hike, though, at the blatant interest two teenagers showed in Amme. The two teens—more men, in truth—had their gazes glued to her backside.

Suddenly he understood Ry's need to growl, a low rumble of displeasure building in his chest. He caught the attention of one teen and winged him a black scowl. The kid elbowed his friend and hurriedly moved down the beach.

"I saw that," Amme said.

"Saw what?"

"The demonstration of ownership."

Crap. "I—"

"I always wondered how Camryn felt when Ry pulled his possessive act. Now I know. It makes me feel special, as if you care." She reached over and pinched his biceps. "Don't do it too often. Now and then works for you. Overdoing will make it lose impact."

Marcus knew his mouth was opening and shutting more than usual and not a squeak emerged. Confusion. Amme tangled his brain in knots. He wanted her, naked and willing in his arms, yet this outing with her and her friends rated as a fun experience too.

"Oh," he managed finally while trying to get his mind around the fact sex had always been the end goal for him. Something in Amme had made that change.

"Do you go out with women often?"

A trick question? He hesitated.

"Just curious. Autumn, do you want to practice your swimming? Try to float between the waves. I'll stand here, and you float to your daddy."

Their skin resembled prunes on exiting the water, but everyone wore broad smiles. While Amme took care of Autumn, Marcus dried himself off and grabbed his wallet.

"I'll go and buy Autumn a hat," he said.

"Thank you," Amme said, and he experienced the tightening of his chest again.

It seemed as if she cared for his daughter. She dried her carefully and applied the suntan lotion Max handed over.

"Camryn, will you keep an eye on Luke for me?" Max asked. "I fancy an ice cream. I'll go with Marcus and bring back ice cream for everyone."

"I'll be careful with him, Max," Camryn said.

"I know you will," Max said, his face softening as he regarded his twin.

"Can we build one of those sandcastle things?" Kaya asked.

Max laughed while puzzlement filled Marcus. At least he'd have a chance to grill Max and find answers to some of his questions.

He waited until they'd crossed the road before he started. "Amme says she's from Romania. Do her friends come from there too?"

"As far as I know." Max's expression turned impassive, the equivalent of those Marcus saw during tough business negotiations. This look screamed knowledge.

"Is that where Camryn has been?"

"She's been with her friends."

Max's words—cagey—and his imagination raced with

possibilities.

"Sometimes they speak in weird clicks and grunts."

"They do?"

"Come on, Max. I'm not stupid. Something doesn't add up here."

"They're good people, Marcus." Max stopped walking and met him head-on with determination. "When Camryn left, her life was on a downward spiral. She was depressed and drinking way too much. Hell, she was an alcoholic. She almost set the barn on fire, and she let Luke wander onto the training track while responsible for watching him. She slept around and pulled all-nighters. I was ready to commit her to a clinic. That's how bad things were. Now, she's clean, and she's got a good man in her life. It's easy to see he loves her. Their friends..." He shrugged. "Sometimes they're a bit odd, but they have each other's backs, and that means a lot to me. They've given me back my sister."

"Wait. You said Camryn was an alcoholic. She was drinking wine yesterday."

"I know," Max said, moving again with long ground-eating strides. "She's perfectly healthy now and seems to manage a few drinks without losing control. It's a miracle, one I intend to enjoy instead of questioning. I'll get ice creams. You want one?"

"Sure. I need to focus on buying a hat. Any idea what a girl would want?"

"Nope." Max laughed, and the bark of sound bore a huge streak of humor. "You're on your own there, mate."

Back at the beach, Marcus handed over the straw hat with trepidation. A bunch of tiny pink and white flowers decorated the brim. He figured even if it was a bit big, it wouldn't matter. They'd make it work.

Autumn gazed at the hat with wonder lighting up her tiny features. "I love it," she said and promptly ran over to Amme to show her the hat. Relief rushed from him along with his held breath.

"Job done," Max said, slapping him on the back. "Who's for ice cream?"

"Me. Me!" Luke said.

"I got your favorite lemon ice pops," Max said to his son. "Here you go. One for Autumn too."

"I'll take ice creams to the castle builders." Marcus carried the bag down the beach to the water's edge. "Ice creams. Time for a break."

"Thanks," Camryn said, accepting one first.

Her friends took the ice creams he offered, but they waited and watched what Camryn did with hers before they followed suit.

"Good choice, Marcus," Camryn said. "I haven't had one of these for years." She took a delicate bite. "Delicious chocolate coating."

"Yum, chocolate," Kaya said and took a huge bite. She took a second bite before she'd swallowed the first. Suddenly, she groaned and held her head. She spat out the ice cream. "Stop! Don't eat it. It's poison. Ow, my head." She glared at Marcus. "What have you done to me?"

Camryn started laughing, and Kaya whirled to face her friend, her fingers pressing into her head. Beside her, Jannike howled and dropped her ice cream on her lap. She pushed at her head. Camryn laughed harder, and Ry and the others stared at their ice creams in suspicion.

"Brain freeze." Fascinated, Marcus scanned their faces. Kaya's hair appeared extra blue today, so bright it almost dazzled his eyes. He was sure the color hadn't been so vibrant earlier. "It happens sometimes when you eat cold foods. The blood vessels in your head are constricting and trying to preserve the heat in your body. It will pass. Lick the roof of your mouth to warm up your soft palate." He lapped at his ice cream to stop it from dripping.

Camryn chortled and took another bite of hers.

"I'm really not dying?" Kaya asked, still rubbing her head.

"No, you can read about it when we get home," Camryn said with a smirk. "You've wasted half of your ice cream. It's chocolate in the middle. Yum!"

Kaya growled and bared her teeth, and Camryn sprang to her feet and hid behind Ry.

"I'm not sharing," Camryn said.

"This chocolate is yummy." Gweneth nibbled on her ice cream, savoring each bite.

Marcus's gaze moved on before returning. "Gweneth, you have sand or mud on your cheek."

Her left hand shot up to the exact spot. Weird. He glanced at Mogens. The man's features were pure white. His gaze shot back to Camryn and found her watching him.

"Mogens, you need some more suntan lotion to stop from burning," she said calmly.

"What?" Mogens glanced at his arm. "Oh, I see what you mean."

"I'll get it," Jannike said. "Is it in your bag?"

"Yes," Mogens said. "The salt water must have washed it off. I didn't factor that into my salve."

"Race you up the beach," Jannike said and took off.

"You're going to lose," Ry said. "She'll never let you hear the end of it."

"Right," Marcus said. He sprinted up the beach, but his mind wasn't in the race. It was stuck back down at the sand castle with Camryn and her friends. He wasn't imagining their oddities. And he suspected Max knew the answers, except he wasn't talking.

Marcus plopped onto his towel and opened his ice cream. Feeling the weight of a stare, he glanced up to find himself the center of Amme's attention.

"Something wrong?" he asked.

"Funny, but I was going to ask you the same thing," she said.

CHAPTER SIX

ONE WEEK LATER

"I like Christmas," Autumn said.

"Me too," Amme agreed with a fervent air.

Camryn laughed and whisked another tray of chocolate chip cookies into the oven. "You both have chocolate spread from one side of your mouth to the other. I was lucky to get enough dough to make the cookies with you two around."

"When can we decorate our Christmas cake?" Gweneth asked.

"So impatient." Camryn tut-tutted. "It needs to cool. We'll do the frosting tomorrow. But I can show you how to make fondant snowmen and Christmas trees to go on top of the cake."

"I want to decorate the chocolate cupcakes," Kaya said. "You said we can make the ones we saw in the shop, the ones with the white chocolate twirls."

Jannike nodded. "Me too."

"I want to do everything," Autumn said in her little girl voice.

"What she said," Kaya said, her head bob-bob-bobbing like Luke at his most excited. All Kaya required was the arm waves, and they'd make creditable twins.

Warmth shimmered through Amme. When Gweneth's father had offered Gweneth's hand in marriage to the winner of the Dowry Derby, Amme had expected to remain on the planet Ornum, at least until her charge wed. That hadn't happened. Ry's hell-horse had won the race, and Amme's life had changed in a heartbeat because he refused to mate with Gweneth. Instead, he'd offered to take Gweneth with them. Amme had traveled with the crew of the Indy because she'd wanted to keep Gweneth safe. She'd never expected to find personal happiness during the process.

"I think Marcus needs a translator. Nanu keeps forgetting to speak his English," Amme said. "Marcus is clever. He's noticing."

"Max said Marcus questioned him, but he put him off." Camryn checked the oven timer. "Ry and I discussed this. We think it's better if we don't tell him. I'll send Mogens over with a translator later tonight. That's the easiest way to divert suspicion."

"I'm keeping him distracted," Amme said, the smugness in her voice making her friends chuckle.

"How many sleeps until Christmas?" Autumn asked.

Amme counted the days on the nearby calendar, proud of the Earth knowledge she'd amassed under pressure. "Twelve sleeps."

"That's a lot of sleeps," Autumn said.

"We have lots to do," Camryn said. "We have to choose a Christmas stocking for you so you're ready for Santa Claus. We have a play date with Luke tomorrow. Max is bringing him over to swim in the pool."

"Can we visit the 'pacas?" Autumn asked.

"You need to ask your daddy," Amme said.

"Ask him what?" Marcus asked. "It smells good in here."

"Chocolate chip cookies," Ry said, entering behind him. "I'm sure that's what I can smell."

Camryn went straight to him, and Amme wished she had the freedom to do the same with Marcus. She forced herself to remain at the kitchen counter. He wasn't a child, and she shouldn't experience this compulsion to keep him safe. She frowned inwardly, testing her system, analyzing. No, not the same response she experienced with Autumn. Similar, true, but different in that she wanted to spend time with him, be with him, and bask in his smile.

"Camryn will smack your hand with a spoon," Autumn said without warning.

"Why?" Marcus asked, cookie in hand.

"You're not meant to steal the cookies yet."

"Busted," Camryn said, waving her wooden spoon at him. "But I think they've probably cooled enough. Anyone want cookies and milk?"

"I'll make a pot of tea," Amme said, and a tremor of pleasure tore through her when Marcus smiled at her with thanks.

"What's on the schedule for tomorrow?" Marcus asked.

"Camryn is going to teach us to sing some Christmas carols. Something about deers while we decorate the Christmas cake," Kaya said. "Does a Christmas cake contain chocolate?"

"No." Camryn pointed at Kaya with her spoon. "You're putting on weight. Even Mogens has noticed your arse is getting bigger. And he was muttering about clouds and readings."

Kaya peered behind at her shorts-clad butt and scowled. "Does my arse look big in this?"

"Yes," her friends chorused.

Marcus just stared because he had no idea what they were talking about. Kaya wasn't fat, and there wasn't a cloud in the sky today.

"We're going to sing a Santa Claus song," Autumn said.

"We also need to do some S. A. N. T. A. shopping," Amme said, spelling the word just as Camryn had told her she should. "We're going to buy a Christmas stocking for Autumn to hang near the fireplace."

Marcus frowned. "Where do we get one of those?"

"Max said there is a stall at the Farmers' market in Clevedon. We're all going on Sunday morning."

"A market? Where?" He'd seen more of the area in the last two weeks than he'd seen in his entire life. After the beach visit, they'd gone to the Christmas parade. They'd visited Rainbow's End, the fun park, and he'd even gone grocery shopping, where Amme's friends had scurried up and down the aisles, picking up and looking at everything. One night, they'd decorated their trees, and now it seemed he'd be participating in carol singing and shopping. He waited for the shudder of horror to sweep through him like a black fog of doom.

It didn't arrive. Not a breath of foghorn terror.

"We should have another barbecue tonight and maybe some dancing," he suggested. "I have a volleyball net and a croquet set somewhere. We can set those up."

"Plan," Camryn said.

"You said dancing because you want to cuddle with Amme," Gweneth said. "And you want to kiss her under that mistletoe stuff."

"Busted," Marcus said. "But I'm not going near the mistletoe if Nanu is around."

A guffaw burst from Camryn. "I wish I'd had a camera. The look on your face. And Nanu's face..." Her cheeks turned red as laughter overtook her.

"Daddy." Autumn tugged on his shirt hem. "Can we visit the 'pacas?"

"We can do that," he said, gazing down at his daughter with a smile of wonder. "As soon as we've eaten cookies."

"I haven't enjoyed the Christmas season so much for ages," Marcus said.

Amme's hands paused on the hem of her T-shirt. She had the translator from Mogens, which she needed to attach behind his ear. A simple enough process.

"I'm glad," she said. "You're making it special for Autumn, too, at a time when she needs more attention than usual. You're lucky you can work from home."

"I lucked out when I found you," he said. "I wouldn't have known what to do if it wasn't for you and your friends. It's not just the babysitting. It's the simple things like decorating the tree and singing carols. Baking food and teaching her to cook. Those are life skills and things she'll remember with pleasure in the years to come. You're giving her traditions."

But she wouldn't be here to share in Autumn's accomplishments. A bittersweet moment and a reaction she shouldn't experience, given her programming. She swiftly diverted her brain back to the present.

"Your daughter is a beautiful child. I can see when she's sad about her mother, and I try to keep her busy. We're going to fit in a movie day with a lunch meal at a restaurant."

"During school holidays?"

"Camryn said that's half the fun. I think she mentioned a Christmas movie. And Kaya heard about a new chocolate shop. She wants to visit. Camryn said we'd need to go too because Kaya requires supervision."

"True, the woman should be the size of a bus with all the chocolate she stuffs into her mouth. I'm in. Give me details, and I'll fit it into my schedule." Marcus held out a hand, his gaze glowing with sensual promise. "Come to bed."

"I'll just peek in on Autumn." Amme hurried off and found Autumn sound asleep. She was a good kid, although she'd had to unleash her anti-monster spray a couple of times when the child

SHELLEY MUNRO

woke with bad dreams.

She found Marcus in bed, the sheet draped across his waist while he checked email on his tablet. He muttered a curse and jabbed at an email to make it disappear.

"Problem?"

"Nothing I can't handle. She asleep?"

"Yes."

He set his tablet aside. "Come here."

Amme paused to whisk off her clothes, and she basked under his intense gaze as she stripped.

"God, you're beautiful," he whispered.

"I like looking at you too."

"Enough with the looking," he said. "I want action."

Amme slid into his arms and sought his lips. Their kisses were no longer hesitant since they'd become comfortable together. And each time, the sex felt better and more satisfying.

She'd placed the translator on the tip of her finger, and now, she clasped Marcus close and strummed a finger over the smooth patch of skin behind his ear. She tapped the translator into place and muttered a few words in the Universal language they spoke.

"I want you too," Marcus replied.

Amme smiled against his lips, sinking into his voracious kiss. Their tongues stroked, dipped, and delved while their hands wandered over shoulders and chests. At least if Nanu slipped now, Marcus wouldn't realize.

Marcus rolled over, taking her with him. She ended up on top of him and stared down at him in surprise.

"I want to see your breasts and watch you when you come."

"So I shouldn't turn off the light?" Amme teased.

"No," he barked. "Loosen your hair. It's so pretty flowing around your shoulders. Smells good too."

"Bossy."

"Hurry, or I'll spank you."

Amme stilled, her heart-pump beating on the fast, choppy side. "Ry threatens to do that to Camryn."

"You think I wouldn't follow through?"

Amme's pulse quickened as she attempted to read him. A sultrier, dangerous mood slithered into the room along with his reply. "I... You always do what you promise."

"Exactly, and don't forget it." He ran a finger down her nose and back and forth across her lips. "I'd enjoy seeing your backside turn pink after I applied my hand."

"Smacking hurts."

"It might at first, but if the smacking is done right, the pain transforms to sensual heat, which makes for very good sex."

"You say that as if you have experience." The translator made it easier for her to express herself.

"I've had sex with other women. I've never said I was a monk. You've been with other men. You told me spanking makes sex better."

"Yes, I have." Which meant she had no right to the squirmy, uncomfortable emotions of jealousy. She'd have to ask Camryn, but she was sure this was the sensation banding her chest and forcing her heart-pump to overcompensate.

"I don't like knowing that," Marcus said, blunt and uncompromising. "It makes me a bastard, but I hate the idea of another man touching you."

The conversation needed turning. "I'm here with you now. We should make the most of it. Let's shove our pasts out of the bed and concentrate on now, on us." She trailed her fingers over his pectoral muscles and pinched one of his nipples. To her fascination, the disc pebbled hard, in a similar way to hers. She pinched the other one to make sure before moving her attentions down his body.

His stomach muscles bunched beneath her fingertips.

"Are you ticklish?"

"No." His hand settled on her hip. "Your skin is extra soft. So sexy. I love touching you."

"You're not soft." Her hand curled around his cock and lightly squeezed. She dipped her head and licked across the fat crown with brief forays underneath. Back and forth and underneath until the tip started to leak with his arousal.

"God, that feels good. No, don't stop. Keep going."

Amme had no idea who this god was, but she continued to explore and tease, giving him a gentle suction of her mouth. His hips lifted, the action forcing him deeper. He groaned, the sound stirring her to drag more of the cries from deep in his throat. She palmed the heavy weight of his testicles and sucked his cock a little harder.

"Amme. I'm gonna come. Take me inside you. Ride me."

Amme repositioned her body and guided him to her. She sank down, taking it slow, teasing both of them with the unhurried penetration.

"Oh, that does feel good. You're deeper than usual." She swayed back and forth until she found the best angle. She rose and fell, her gaze on Marcus and the enjoyment etched into his hard features. When she didn't get enough friction, she used her finger and stroked her pleasure center.

"That looks so damn hot," Marcus said in a hoarse voice.

Her inner muscles clenched around his shaft, and he groaned, his brown eyes glittering with mesmerizing golden highlights, with excitement and enthusiasm. His hips strained upward, surging deep into her pussy. Strained breathing and soft sighs resounded inside the bedroom, the scent of sex and Marcus's citrus aftershave filling her senses.

A coil of energy surged to her lower body, the ball of heat growing larger and larger with each up and down stroke. The pleasure swelled until she didn't think her body could contain the blissful sensations or continue the urgent tempo.

Marcus reached up and pinched her nipple. The spike of pain

surprised her and shoved her into an emotional storm. Her orgasm ripped through her, hard and intense, her pussy pulsing around his cock.

"Hey, beautiful."

Amme realized she'd stopped to grab her own pleasure, and a spurt of concern dulled some of her enjoyment. "Sorry, I stopped moving."

Marcus rolled until she lay under him. "Not a problem."

His kiss stopped her reply, her explanation. His was hot and hungry, and when he parted their lips, not a single thought of regret remained. His potent power claimed her, leaving a heavy fog of desire shimmering in the air between them.

He set up a fast rhythm until all she could do was hold on and enjoy the ride. He drove into her again, and another mini-explosion rocked her system.

Marcus groaned. "Amme." And then he was coming, her receptors recognizing the convulsive heave of his muscles and the spurt of semen from his cock. For an instant she felt his full body weight and luxuriated in the sensation, which too quickly ended. He levered off her and pulled free.

"Fuck," he muttered. "We didn't use a condom."

Amme stilled at the note in his voice. She met his gaze without flinching, simply staring at him.

"Fuck," he said again and stomped away. He disappeared into the en suite, leaving Amme hurt and confused. Was the idea so abhorrent?

He returned mins later.

"Do you want me to go?"

He ignored the question. "How likely are you to get pregnant?"

Amme fought hard to remain impassive, but her receptors sent signals before her brain override them. Her mouth shaped into a twist, into the grimace they called a scowl here on Earth. She'd thought he'd cared a little, but the note in his voice, the horrified attitude, said otherwise.

"Amme?" The bark of her name was an order.

"I won't get pregnant." The weird ache commenced behind her eyes and she blinked slowly, then faster. Neither speed helped.

"Are you on birth control?"

"No."

"Then how do you know."

Amme's heart-pump stuttered, taking an extra long pause before the next push of mechanics. She climbed off the bed, the atmosphere in the room prickling across her skin in an icy chill. She scooped up her T-shirt and pulled it over her head, the barrier of clothing steadying her again.

"Amme."

"Don't worry, Marcus. I am unable to have children." She bent to collect the rest of her clothes and left his bedroom without looking back.

Fuck. Marcus dragged a hand through his hair and dropped onto his bed. That had gone well. While he'd panicked, she'd become increasingly colder, her whiskey eyes filling with an expression that skirted—no—it was bloody contempt.

He bent at the waist and covered his face with his hands. He'd screwed up. Amme hadn't deserved his icy behavior. Time for an apology.

Marcus stood and padded from the room. Damn, he needed clothes. He retraced his steps and pulled on a pair of jeans. Dressed enough.

He tapped softly on Amme's door, and when she didn't answer, he opened it and peered inside the room. The bed was empty, the room vacant.

Panic struck him then. She couldn't leave. He...he... He raced for the stairs, then came to an abrupt halt. She wouldn't leave Autumn. He knew this bone deep.

On leaving his room, she would've gone to Autumn to check she was all right. He paused at the door and heard low voices. His daughter was awake at...he frowned at his watch...2:00 a.m.

"The monster was making noises. I h-heard it run under the bed." Autumn made a hiccupping sound. "You need to l-look."

"All right, sweetie," Amme said in a reassuring voice. "Don't worry. I'll get the anti-monster spray. The biggest, baddest monster can't withstand my spray gun."

"You need to do your dance."

"I'll do that too," Amme said. "Let me look first. You might have already scared the beast away."

Marcus listened to the two discuss monsters and thought back to his own childhood. His nanny had comforted him after bad dreams. Not his mother or father. They'd never spent much time at home. Heck, they were mostly out of the country these days. Jocelyn and Mark Polo shouldn't have had children, hadn't wanted them.

With their parents as examples, it was no wonder he and Olivia had ended up with commitment issues. Well, in his case at least. His much younger sister acted out with outrageous antics in a cry for attention.

"I was right," Amme said. "You have chased the monster away. It's not hiding under the bed. You're a monster slayer!"

"It's gone?"

"Yes. Excellent job. I'll spray now, so it won't come back."

Marcus heard the swish-swish of a spray bottle. Then Amme stood and jumped around singing nonsensical words. Something clenched in the region of his heart. Amme would make a brilliant mother. Autumn adored her, and Amme's presence had helped his daughter at a time when her mother's death could have paralyzed her. For a person who so obviously adored children, not being able to have her own must be a constant ache in her gut.

"Damn," he mumbled.

Amme's head shot up, and their gazes met. She was the first to break their connection.

"Now that the monster is gone, you should go back to sleep because we have an exciting day tomorrow. I'll tuck you in."

"I can't find Teddy."

"Here he is. He'd fallen out of bed." Amme tucked the stuffed animal next to Autumn and kissed his daughter on the forehead. "Sweet dreams."

Amme brushed past him, her destination the bedroom he'd allocated her when she'd first arrived—the one she'd seldom used.

"Amme." His arm shot out to halt her retreat. "Please, can we talk?"

"I thought we'd said everything that needed saying."

"I'm sorry for the way I behaved. You didn't deserve my attitude."

"Or the way you implied I'd try to trap you. I'm leaving with my friends, remember?"

Damn, it wasn't as if he could forget her looming departure. He gritted his teeth, strove for the right words. Trust was—the more he thought about her leaving, the more he loathed the idea. He liked the way he was with her. She'd helped him find his feet with Autumn. And most of all, she didn't care about his money. He'd scanned the items she'd purchased for Autumn, and she hadn't gone to exclusive boutiques. Most of his past women would have hotfooted it to the designer stores and sneaked in several outfits for their own pleasure. Camryn had suggested The Warehouse, a large chain store with reasonable prices, and that was where Amme and her friends had gone. And from the sounds of it, they'd had a blast during their shopping excursion.

"I know," he said in a low voice. "I apologize for letting my past color my reaction. You didn't deserve that."

"I would never try to trap a man into marriage," Amme said with dignity. "Good night. I'll see you in the morning."

And before he could offer a protest, Amme opened the door to her allocated bedroom and disappeared inside. The loud click of the door closing was her rejection.

"That went well." Marcus dragged a hand through his hair. He wouldn't sleep. Not now. Maybe he'd check his email and do a little work. That way, he'd have plenty of time to think about a grovel speech and his next apology.

Down in the kitchen, he shifted his unopened mail to get to his whiskey bottle and poured himself a shot. Immediately, he thought of Amme and her beautiful eyes. If he weren't such an idiot, he'd be in bed with her instead of standing in the kitchen alone.

A heavy sigh rumbled up his throat. He sipped his drink, scooped up his pile of mail then wandered along to his office and settled in to do some work.

He opened a couple of farm bills. Feed for the alpacas and a vet bill. A small padded parcel snagged his attention. He yanked off the tape and slid out the contents—a pair of silky underwear. Aw, hell. Sophie Robinson strikes again. He'd thought his warnings and his abrupt statement of disinterest would finally get through to the determined female. Apparently not. He dropped the panties in his bin along with the rest of the parcel's contents.

He grunted, the sound full of displeasure. At least she'd sent a parcel rather than trying to sneak into his house and bed. Been there. Done that, and he didn't care for a repeat.

Hell, he was an idiot.

Amme was a hundred miles from Sophie and the women who'd tried to insert themselves into his life because of his money. And Amme was nothing like his child-neglecting parents.

A click came from the direction of the kitchen.

Amme.

Relief surged inside him, and he tossed aside the rest of his mail. He hurried into the kitchen, his bare feet soundless on the tile floor. Someone—not Amme—was busy raiding his fridge.

"Stop right there," he snarled.

The person let out a very feminine squeak and dropped a bottle of milk. Marcus reached for the light and blinked at the sudden brightness.

The woman pivoted, her rainbow-colored hair unfamiliar. Her defiant blue eyes, outlined in heavy black eyeliner, and the dark lashes, long and thick and partly man-made had him relaxing.

"Olivia," he said in exasperation. "What are you doing here?"

A flash of movement came from the other side of the kitchen. Amme dressed in a sexy bronze-colored gown that came to mid-thigh. Her arm lifted, and a shocked croak crawled up his throat, boasted by a slice of panic.

"It's all right," he said hastily. Hell, where had she found the club?

Amme scowled at the woman and the weapon didn't move.

Crap.

"Amme, this is my sister, Olivia."

"She couldn't enter in the normal fashion?" Amme's arm finally dropped to her side. "At a reasonable hour?"

"What did she say?" Olivia asked, turning to Amme. "What language— Whoa! Don't hit me with that. Marcus, tell her I'm your sister."

"It's true," Marcus said. "Olivia is my sister."

Amme's cool gaze slid from him to Olivia and back. "I'll leave you two to catch up. I'm going back to bed."

"No, you don't have to leave."

Amme lifted her nose a fraction before she glided away. Both he and Olivia stared after her until she disappeared from sight.

"Well," Olivia said. "Things have changed if you have a live-in girlfriend."

"What are you doing here?" Amme had spoken plain English. Had Olivia been drinking?

Olivia stiffened, a flash of hurt showing before her expression blanked. "Where else is there to go?"

"Sorry, let me rephrase that. Mum and Dad said you were spending Christmas with a friend in France." He scanned her features. No, his sister appeared perfectly sober.

Olivia ducked her gaze before lifting it again. This time, she radiated a clear challenge. "It didn't work out."

"Why?"

"Her brother made a pass at me. He wouldn't take no for an answer, and when I kneed him in the balls, the blame got pushed to me. Janet's parents kicked me out."

"How did you get to New Zealand?"

"I flew to Heathrow and caught an Air New Zealand flight home. Please don't send me back to the finishing school." Her chin lifted in her usual belligerent manner, and sympathy rushed through him. He hadn't been a good big brother so far, but that could change.

"You can stay here. We'll talk about the future later."

"Really?"

Marcus grinned. "Really. Let's get this mess cleaned up and I'll show you to the guest room."

Olivia bent down and picked up the empty milk bottle. "Can't I use the same one I used last time I was here?"

"Nope, my daughter Autumn has that room."

Olivia gaped at him again. "You're married?"

He grinned again, the curve of his lips feeling extra big and wide. "No. It's a long story. I'll tell you while you eat. I'll get a mop. What?" he asked when his sister gaped at him.

"You've changed. You're not so intense and aggressive. You look happy."

"I am happy." Nothing less than the truth, he realized. Autumn's arrival in his life, and Amme's, had shifted his attitude and made him take a hard look at his life. He didn't need to work as hard as he did. Delegation was working just fine.

"Who's the woman?"

"Amme. She's looking after Autumn."

"Pretty sexy lingerie for a babysitter."

Busted. "So?"

Olivia grinned and appeared years younger despite the black eyeliner and matching lipstick. "She isn't your normal type."

"She's not," he said. "I like her very much. She's visiting with Max's sister, Camryn. You remember my neighbor, Max. Did you meet him? I'm sure I told you about him—the one who trains racehorses."

"The hottie."

"The married hottie," Marcus said. "His twin sister and her friends are here until the New Year. We're having Christmas dinner here since Max and Ellen are off to Taupo."

"That sounds lame," Olivia said.

Little did she know. It was anything but lame, and Marcus decided he wouldn't elaborate. He'd let Olivia discover Amme's friends on her own. "I'll get that mop."

"You want a cup of tea?"

"Sure." He disappeared into the utility room and found the mop and bucket.

When he returned, Olivia put on the kettle and cleaned up some of the mess she'd created on the counter. He started mopping up the milk.

"Are you going to tell Mum and Dad?"

"Only if they ring asking questions," Marcus said.

Olivia wrinkled her nose. "That's not very likely."

"No," he agreed. "Their loss."

"Thank you, Marcus. I thought you might be angry."

"Nah, Amme is the angry one tonight."

"Why?"

"We had a situation," he said finally. He was not telling his twenty-year-old sister that, in the heat of the moment, he'd forgotten to use birth control. He'd never hear the end of her laughing jeers.

"No details?"

"Not a one."

Olivia poured the water into the teapot. "Is she a keeper?"

"It's starting to look that way," he confessed, and the idea didn't panic him as it had earlier.

"Curiouser and curiouser," Olivia said. "I can't wait to meet Amme properly. Autumn too. Are you sure she's yours?"

"She's got the same Polo-colored hair and my eyes." He shot a look at the rainbow of Olivia's spiky do. "Same color as me anyway. I'll get a DNA test done in the new year, but I'm not expecting any surprises."

"What about her mother?"

"She's dead. Cancer."

"Rough," Olivia said. "Do Mum and Dad know?"

"Not yet. I haven't spoken to them since they left for New York."

"Me neither," Olivia said. "Sure makes you feel the love, huh? The decorations are gorgeous. Both the homemade and the store bought ones. I saw the tree when I came in. The red and silver looks great in your lounge."

"Amme's friends wanted a tree, and I didn't have the heart to say no. I'm glad I didn't. It's been fun. They're staying in the cottage. You'll meet them in the morning."

After they finished cleaning up, they drank their tea in companionable silence. He watched his sister, witnessed her inner battle.

"What is it?" he asked.

"I don't want to go back to school. Learning to walk with a book balanced on my head is boring."

The last time he'd seen his sister, she'd worn her autumn-colored hair long. This bright explosion of color and the shaggy style wasn't in the least bit boring. "Did the school approve of your new hairstyle?"

"No. I ended up with detention for a week."

"What do you want to do?"

Olivia shrugged. "I don't know. The only thing I've learned at the school is that I don't want to marry a wealthy man and fill the position of society wife."

Marcus spluttered out a laugh as he eyed his sister. In her short T-shirt, black leather jacket, and jeans with strategic rips, she looked nothing like a debutant. When he factored in the hair and the makeup, he thought she'd work as an MC princess. Not that he intended to inform her of this opinion.

"There's no hurry," he said. "Stay here for Christmas and the New Year. Longer if you want. We'll work out something."

She sniffed, and he lifted his hands to ward her off.

"You're not gonna cry?"

She chuckled—a watery gurgle—then yawned. "Nope. Man, I'm tired. I flew nonstop with a four-hour layover in LA."

Marcus stood. "Come on. I'll show you to your room. Where's your luggage?"

"My bag is just inside the front door."

"Wait there, and I'll grab it."

Ten minutes later, Marcus decided to go to bed himself. He fell asleep for a while but woke again an hour later. He missed Amme.

CHAPTER SEVEN

CHRISTMAS EVE

Amme didn't sleep well, and before she considered the early hour, she commed Camryn.

"What's up?" Camryn asked, her tone thick with fatigue.

"Sorry. Did I wake you?"

"It's okay. Just a sec, let me put the com on speaker so Ry can hear."

"No!" Amme blurted. "I don't want to talk to Ry. Just you."

"Oh?"

Amme prowled across the floor of her bedroom and turned to pace back to the bed when she ran out of floor space. "Marcus didn't use a condom last night."

"But you can't... Oh," Camryn said. "I guess the conversation became sticky."

"I saw his reaction. He thought I was trying to trap him."

"Did he say that?"

"No, he tried to apologize, but I moved back to my room."

"What do you want to do?"

"I want him to trust me," Amme said. "I like him."

"Oh, Amme." Compassion filled her friend's voice. "We're leaving at the beginning of January."

"Don't you think I know that? I keep telling myself we have no future, but...but..." Amme blinked to stop the weird tingling currently messing with her vision. "That's not all. I'm sure I'm malfunctioning. My heart-pump keeps going too fast. My sight goes blurry at the oddest moments. And my receptors seem to be faulty. Remember I told you my system attaches to a child, and I feel a compulsion to look after them and keep them safe?"

"Yes," Camryn said.

"Well, I'm getting the same compulsion with Marcus. My tronics need a service."

Camryn snorted out an abrupt laugh. It stopped mid-sound as if she'd slapped a hand over her mouth.

"It's not funny."

"Amme, I'm sorry. I'm not laughing at you. Well, I am, but in a good way. I think you've fallen in love with Marcus."

"What?" No. "It isn't possible."

"Think about it. You have the same symptoms I had with Ry. Apart from the tattoo business. That's what falling in love feels like. Your pulse races. Your emotions go up and down. You're in love with Marcus."

"Well, it's annoying. How do I self-correct?"

Camryn chuckled. "Unfortunately, that's not an option. Don't worry. We have a lot to keep us busy. We'll keep your mind off Marcus. Should Ry and I come for breakfast?"

"Yes." Amme didn't think for one min Camryn was right, but it wouldn't hurt to have her friend—all her friends—around to act as a buffer. She issued a heavy sigh as she disconnected the com to

Camryn. Never had two weeks seemed so long.

Marcus was up early, despite approving of a Sunday morning lie in. Might as well get up now because he wasn't sleeping. He dressed in shorts and a T-shirt and checked on Autumn. She was awake.

"Hi, sweetheart. Do you want to get dressed?"

She nodded. "You need to do my hair." She shot him an uncertain—no, doubtful glance, one that pricked at his ego. "I want pigtails."

He found her clothes—a bright pink T-shirt and denim shorts—and even managed to brush and bunch her hair into pigtails as per her little girl instructions. Bossy much? She probably got that from him.

"Do we need to do anything else?"

"No. Where's Amme?"

"Amme is sleeping late today."

The color fled from her cheeks. "Is she sick?"

Hell. He sought to reassure her. "No, she's not sick. My sister arrived last night, and we all stayed up late. Your aunt."

"I have an aunt?"

"Yes, Aunt Olivia is looking forward to meeting you."

"Is she sleeping?"

"Yes. We'll see both Amme and Aunt Olivia when they wake up."

This was the first time he'd spent so much time with Autumn, and he found himself unaccountably nervous. Him—the man who wielded so much power in the business world. Part of him wanted to chortle at himself. Frightened of a little girl.

"I feel like pancakes today."

She wrinkled her cute nose. "Do you know how to make pancakes?"

"Ye of little faith." They entered the kitchen. "Why don't you sit up here at the breakfast counter, and I'll show you how to make pancakes."

Marcus set the coffee going first and poured Autumn a glass of juice before he started on the pancakes. Pretty easy since he had a packet of mix in the pantry. Adding milk and egg didn't take much brainpower. He paused, suspecting Amme's friends would arrive for breakfast, and tipped in more mix. In five minutes flat, he had the first one sitting in front of Autumn.

"Do you want syrup?"

"I don't know," she said.

"I'll show you how I make mine, but you can put on any topping you want. Your Aunt Olivia used to eat hers with ice cream."

"But you can't have ice cream at morning time."

"I know, but your Aunt Olivia is naughty."

"Hey! I heard that," Olivia said.

Autumn turned to study his sister, her mouth pursing on seeing Olivia's hair.

"Olivia, this is Autumn," Marcus said.

Olivia grinned. "You look just like me when I was younger, except you have Marcus's eyes."

A small frown grew on Autumn's brow. She glanced at him then at his sister. "Will my hair go like that?"

Marcus barked out a laugh.

"Hey, what's wrong with my hair?" Olivia demanded, but amusement stretched her mouth wide in a toothy smile.

"You have rainbow hair," Autumn said.

A rapid tap came and then footsteps sounded. More than one set.

"That will be Amme's friends. Grab some plates and cutlery, will ya? I'll get the cereal and coffee mugs," Marcus said.

"Morning," Gweneth said, her steps slowing when she didn't see Amme. "Where's Amme?"

Nanu bumped into the back of her and grabbed Gweneth before she fell.

"Still asleep," Marcus said. "This is my sister Olivia."

"We made some muffins," Kaya said, striding into the kitchen, carrying a container. "Blueberry. Cool hair."

"This is my sister Olivia," Marcus said again. "Anyone for pancakes?"

"What are pancakes?" Jannike asked.

Marcus was becoming used to their questions and equally convinced none of them had ever set foot in Romania. "Autumn is eating the first one."

They all peered at Autumn's plate.

"Yes, please," Mogens said.

In a well-synchronized procedure, Amme's friends set the table and added the contributions they'd brought with them. Gweneth handed him a mug of coffee, doctored with a dash of milk, just as he liked it. She put on another pot while Nanu took care of Autumn's needs, the big man with beaded dreads at ease with the small girl.

Olivia sidled up to him as he cooked pancakes. "You have a family," she whispered, and there was a wistful note in her voice.

She was right. Marcus didn't know how it had happened, but he felt comfortable with Amme and her friends. They helped each other, each of them pulling their weight in different ways.

"I love the tree and the decorations," Olivia said.

Another tap sounded at the door.

"It's Camryn and Ry," Kaya said without even turning.

He was becoming used to their intuitive remarks too. They each seemed to possess spidey senses. Disconcerting at first, but now he didn't so much as blink an eye.

"Morning," Camryn said. "Where's Amme?"

"Still upstairs. This is Olivia, my sister," Marcus said.

"I'll take over cooking," Camryn said. "You go and see if she's all right." She seized the spatula out of his hand and edged him out of the way.

Marcus hesitated then strode from the kitchen. He wanted to

see Amme.

Her bedroom was empty, the bed neatly made. He found her in Autumn's room, busily making the bed and sorting laundry.

"Amme, I'm sorry," he burst out. "I was stupid and insensitive, and I couldn't sleep without you in my arms. Please forgive me."

She studied him for a long moment until he wanted to fidget. "I don't wish to argue either," she said finally. "I will leave soon, and I don't wish to waste the time fighting with you."

Relief charged through him, leaving him strangely breathless. He was at her side in two giant steps and swept her into his arms. His lips met hers, and he didn't let her go for a long, long time.

"There is something strange about Amme and her friends," Olivia said. "Sometimes they communicate in weird clicks and grunts, usually when I'm not in the room with them. And even weirder, sometimes you're there when they do it, and you seem to understand them."

Marcus frowned and pulled up outside his parents' house in Remuera, a suburb of Auckland, not far from the city center. "I noticed the weird language when they first arrived, but I haven't heard it for weeks now. Autumn always seems to understand them."

"They don't come from Romania," Olivia said. "Do you have a key for the house? I can't find mine."

"Sure, there's one on my key ring. I asked my neighbor Max about them. He said he trusted his sister with his life, and although he hadn't met her friends before, if she said they were okay, he wasn't going to ask questions." Marcus unlocked the door, and they stepped into the family home.

Olivia tapped in the security code. "I don't get a dangerous vibe from them, but something is...off."

"They're great with Autumn," Marcus said.

"You're good with her, too," Olivia said. "I couldn't imagine you as a father, but you're great. Autumn is a lucky girl."

Marcus had to clear his throat before he could reply. "If it wasn't for Amme, I wouldn't know what to do. Everything I know, I've learned from her."

"They're leaving on the second of January."

"I know. Every time I think about it, my gut tightens," Marcus said. Things were perfect between him and Amme now. Really good. In fac,t he'd never felt this level of intimacy with anyone else.

"Don't let her go," Olivia said, as if that were the easiest thing in the world. "You know I hesitated about coming to you, but I didn't have anywhere else to go. I'm glad I did. This is the best Christmas I've ever had, and we haven't even had our Christmas Day yet. Have you bought your Secret Santa gift?"

"No, not yet. I thought we might do some quick shopping on the way home. I've ordered something special for Amme, and I need to pick it up." He paused to grin at his sister. "This is the best Christmas I've ever had too. Amme and her friends make it so much fun. Go and pack your stuff, and we can hit the shops before they get crazy busy with last-minute panic shoppers."

Olivia giggled. "That would be us."

"Appears so." Marcus wandered through his parents' house, deep in thought. His phone rang, and he pulled it from his pocket and glanced at the screen. Sophie Robinson. Again. He hesitated then answered. "Sophie, what do you want?"

"I forgive you," she said in a tearful voice. "I forgive you, Marcus, and I want to spend Christmas with you."

"What?" He'd dated her twice and hadn't asked her out a third time because she'd turned into the clingy type.

"I've been invited to the Carricks for lunch and to the Mackintoshs for drinks tonight. I've accepted for both of us," she gushed. "You can pick me up at my apartment. I'll bring a bag so I can stay with you overnight."

"No," Marcus said in a hard voice. "Sophie, I made it plain we weren't suited. I'm seeing someone else. I have a child."

"But I sent you my favorite underwear."

"Unsolicited mail," he snapped. "Don't try to contact me again because I'm not interested." He hung up with a low curse.

"Problem?"

"I dated a woman called Sophie Robinson. Twice. I didn't ask her out a third time because she's a nutter." In the past, he would've brushed off the question from his sister, but he didn't consider censoring himself today. It was a measure of how much closer they'd become—all due to Amme and her friends and his daughter. "She seems to think I'm spending Christmas with her and has accepted invitations on my behalf."

"Have you mentioned it to Amme and the others?"

"No."

"You should, just in case she turns up at your place. If she's a bit weird..." Olivia shrugged. "You never know."

His phone rang. "It's her again."

"Give it to me," Olivia said. "Hello. Is this Sophie? Please leave Marcus alone. He's not interested in you." She hung up and handed over the phone. "You're right. She's weird. Maybe you should report her to the police."

"I don't think it's bad enough to warrant that sort of step. She's harassing me by phone, the odd e-mail, and sending me packages, but that's all. Are you done? We should hit the shops."

"I promised Gweneth I'd give her some makeup tips and help her color her hair," Olivia said. "I need to buy supplies. She gave me some money."

"Just buy the basics, enough to tide her over until tomorrow," Marcus said.

"She's your person in the Secret Santa."

"Maybe," Marcus said, and Olivia offered him a conspiratorial grin and tapped one finger to her nose.

They arrived back at the house to find everyone clustered in small groups with Christmas paper, tape, ribbons and gift tags in evidence. Amme and Autumn were in the kitchen making some sort of cookies or cake. The scent of ginger and cinnamon and allspice scented the air.

"It smells like Christmas in here," Olivia said.

"What's going on?" Marcus asked.

"Everyone is wrapping stuff to go under the tree. They're also sorting out S. A. N. T. A. things for later," Amme said with a nod at his daughter.

"Hello, Daddy." Autumn smiled at him, splotches of chocolate decorating her pink T-shirt and her chin. His chest squeezed tight with pleasure, and he grinned back.

"We've been shopping too. I need to make my own wrapping huddle." His phone went, and he cursed inwardly. "Be back in a minute." He seized one of Olivia's bags and his shopping and carried it upstairs, letting the phone go to voice mail. He dropped the bag in Olivia's room and continued to his bedroom. His and Amme's room, he thought with a spurt of pleasure.

The phone rang again. It was Sophie. This time, he switched off the phone and placed it in his bedside drawer. It was Christmas break. Anything work-related would wait, and his mother could ring the house number if she wanted to contact him. Not that he thought it likely. He and Olivia wouldn't hear from them until they arrived home again. They probably didn't even know Olivia had left France.

He vowed then he'd never follow his parents' example when it came to Autumn. He thought of the future, and a spurt of humor zapped him. He intended to be the stern father terrorizing Autumn's boyfriends when she started dating, the doting father at birthdays and special occasions, the encouraging father as she grew to adulthood and spread her wings.

No, he'd never tread the same path. He'd experienced the bite of disappointment when his mother had sent the staff to deal with them instead of coming herself—something he'd never inflict upon his own child.

The days were passing so quickly. Amme rolled gingerbread dough for Autumn, her mind only half on the mindless task. Soon, they'd leave.

"You okay?" Camryn asked.

"I didn't hear you come in," Amme said, blinking from her reverie.

"I know. You looked deep in thought. Anything I can help with?"

"No. Yes. I don't know." Amme gave a helpless shrug.

"Marcus?"

She should admit the truth, at least to herself and her best friend. "I don't want to leave him and Autumn."

"What does Marcus say?"

Amme shot a glance at Autumn, who was listening. "I haven't asked him."

"We'll talk later," Camryn said. "Should I supervise while you do some wrapping?"

"I need to wrap presents," Autumn said.

"Hey, kiddo," Olivia said from the doorway of the kitchen. "Would you like to wrap presents with me, once you're done with the gingerbread men? Maybe I can help here, too. Have you made a cat gingerbread yet? I can make those."

"Luke likes cats," Autumn said.

Camryn chuckled, the sound infectious, and Amme found

herself smiling too.

"A lucky circumstance for me, Autumn," Camryn said.

Amme felt the weight of a stare and caught Olivia's speculative glance. Somehow, they needed to fit her with a translator. Nanu kept forgetting even though they'd started sticking him with kitchen duty each time he used the Universal language. The trouble was they'd all become comfortable here with Marcus and had so much fun they'd relaxed.

"How about we finish this gingerbread and get it in the oven then we can wrap our presents and put them under the tree?" Camryn asked.

Olivia rolled up her sleeves to reveal a tattoo of a spiral tail.

"What's that?" Autumn asked, pointing at Olivia's arm.

"Oops, I've been keeping that hidden so Marcus didn't see," Olivia said and rolled her sleeve back down.

"Didn't see what?" Marcus said.

"Olivia has a tattoo," Camryn said.

Amme remained quiet because she didn't want to say anything dumb.

"What's a tattoo?" Autumn shoved a piece of gingerbread dough into her mouth when everyone focused on Olivia.

Olivia screwed up her nose. "Seems I'm busted. At least I can quit wearing long sleeves. I've been roasting in this summer heat." And with that said, she shrugged out of her shirt to reveal a colorful tattoo in red, blue, black, green and yellow that covered one shoulder and the tail curled around her left biceps.

"A dragon," Camryn said. "It's beautiful work."

"I want one," Autumn said.

"You have to wait until you're at least twenty," Olivia said. "But we can get some that will last for a week if that's all right with your father."

"They do henna ones at the mall," Camryn said. "They last for a couple of weeks. We could all get one after Christmas."

"Yes," Amme said.

Marcus groaned. "Look what you've done, Olivia."

Amme laughed, and the others joined in.

"What's up?" Nanu asked. "Wow, Liv. That's cool." He traced his finger over the colors then inspected the tip of his finger.

"That's a tattoo," Camryn said hurriedly. "The color is set into the skin."

"I want one," Nanu said.

"After Christmas," Camryn said. "But you should know they use needles to make the patterns. It hurts. Also, one like Liv's can take several sessions with the tattoo artist."

"It didn't hurt much," Olivia said and winked at Nanu. "A tough guy like you should be able to handle tattoo needles."

"Course I can. What do we do with our presents now?" Nanu asked.

"Make sure they have names on them, so we know who they're for, then put them under the tree," Camryn said. "If they're S. A. N. T. A. ones, then keep them separate. We'll do something with them tonight."

"Okay," Nanu said, and he walked out singing about Santa Claus coming to town. He halted in the doorway. "I'm going for a swim once this is done. Anyone up for a game of water volleyball?"

There were shouts of assent.

"You go and play, Amme," Olivia said. "I'll finish up here with Autumn and help her with present wrapping."

"Thanks," Amme said and turned to wipe the remnants of dough from her hands.

"I will be the volleyball judge," Mogens said. "A tough job since you all cheat."

Everyone booed and hissed and shouted insults. Amme grinned before hurrying upstairs to change into her bikini.

CHAPTER EIGHT

CHRISTMAS MORNING

"Santa visited," Autumn shouted.

She ran into their room and jumped on the bed, astonishing Marcus. He coughed to clear the tightening of his throat and savored the warm emotion seeping into his chest.

"He ate the gingerbread man and the bottle of beer I left him. My stocking is full."

"Really?" Marcus said.

"You're awake early," Amme said, clutching the sheet to her naked breasts.

"Olivia said I'm allowed on Christmas," Autumn said.

A laugh came from the door, and Marcus spied his sister. "Why don't you get Olivia to help you dress? Amme and I will be down soon."

"No time for a quickie," Olivia warned as she took Autumn's hand and ushered her from the bedroom. "Jannike, Nanu, and Kaya have already gone to Max's farm to help with the chores. Mogens and Gweneth are making breakfast."

"What's a quickie?" Autumn asked.

Marcus groaned even as his sister laughed and shut the door. "I don't care what Olivia says. I'm kissing you good morning. Merry Christmas."

"Merry Christmas, Marcus."

The expression in her beautiful whiskey eyes grabbed him, sent a wave of love soaring through him, and in that moment, he decided he'd ask her to stay when her friends left. He'd ask her to marry him, and he'd propose on New Year's Eve.

He smiled and kissed her, putting his emotions into the exchange. Her arms wound around his neck, and she gave back everything in return. When they finally parted, they were both breathing hard.

"Want a shower before we go down?"

She nodded.

"I'll scrub your back for you."

"Marcus, that will slow us down."

"Too bad," he said and reached for her hand. Best Christmas ever.

Excitement fizzled through Amme as she walked down the stairs. She caught a glimpse of the Christmas tree lights as they passed the lounge, and someone had put on Christmas music. It wafted from concealed speakers, and Mogens and Gweneth sang along.

At the bottom of the stairs, Marcus fell into step with her, holding her close to his side with an arm around her waist. They strolled to the kitchen.

"Champagne?" Gweneth asked.

"Thank you," Amme said.

"Autumn is in the lounge. She refuses to open her stocking until you and Marcus arrive. We'll bring in the champagne," Mogens said, and he radiated the same anticipation simmering in Amme. His skin verged on the extreme side of pale, but he still appeared human.

"At last," Olivia said when they entered the lounge.

Amme took a sec to admire their tree. It was stunning with the red bobbles and glittering white lights. The scent of pine filled the air, along with ginger and spices from the candles Olivia must have lit before they arrived. A man with a husky voice sang about silent nights.

Autumn stood by the wood burner, a bulging red Christmas stocking at her feet. Her weight shifted from foot to foot. She paused to bounce on her toes, and when she saw them, her eyes glowed. She pointed at the stocking and beamed. "Look!"

"We need photos," Olivia said. "Do you have your camera, Marcus?"

"I'll get it." When he returned a few mins later with his camera, his expression was a mask of foreboding.

"Something wrong?" Amme asked, concern taking her to his side.

"No. Everything is fine." He smiled, but she could see it took effort. He snapped several shots, checked the viewing screen. "We're here. Are you going to show us what Santa brought you?"

"Open your stocking," Olivia encouraged. "Never seen a kid so determined to wait. I would have ripped that sucker open hours ago."

Autumn reached inside and pulled out the first item. "Santa has the same wrapping paper as us."

"Why yes! He does," Marcus said, laughter threading through his voice. "He must have bought it on sale at the same shop as us. He probably goes through a lot of paper."

Amme felt the quiver of her mouth as she fought her

amusement. Autumn showed brightness and intelligence, and looking at Marcus and Olivia, Amme knew where at least part of this facet of her personality came from.

Autumn made quick work of the wrapping paper.

"Ooh, look! A coloring book. And some paints." She ripped open another parcel. "Some crayons." She came to a big parcel and made quick work of the paper. "A doll, and look! She has some clothes." She displayed each new item—books, chocolate and a glossy orange with the same excitement. Finally, she glanced up at them, a sea of wrapping paper surrounding her small body. Spots of pink exhilaration shaded her cheeks.

Marcus took several photos, and Amme made herself a promise she'd get copies of these photos. Maybe Camryn had enough money to buy one of those tablets. Nanu was clever. He'd find some way of keeping the thing charged so they could look at the photos and remember their visit to Camryn's family.

A wave of reluctance filled her at the idea of leaving. Oh, they might manage another visit, but years would've passed here on Earth. She wouldn't see Autumn growing up, changing, and blooming into a young woman. That weird achy sensation pushed at her vision, blurring the sharp lines of her surroundings, and her throat tightened. She swallowed, and it subsided, but she made a mental note to ask Mogens to check her systems to make sure her cybernetics were functioning as intended.

"Champagne?" Gweneth asked, motioning to the tray she held.

Marcus took two glasses and handed one to her. When everyone except Autumn had a glass, he lifted his glass. "A toast," he said. "To friends and happiness. Merry Christmas."

"To friends," Mogens said.

"To friends," Amme echoed the others and shifted her mind from their departure in exactly eight days.

Breakfast was underway when Camryn, Ry, and the others arrived. They'd taken showers after their chores and trooped inside en mass.

"Merry Christmas," they chorused.

"I'm starving," Ry said.

"What's for breakfast?" Jannike asked.

"Smells great," Camryn said.

"If Mogens cooked, I'm not eating," Kaya said.

"I helped with the eggs," Mogens said when the others hooted and teased. "I have improved. There are no shells this time. You have toast, though, if you're worried. I'll eat your share."

Family, Amme thought with satisfaction. She ushered everyone to the festive table Olivia had set and helped Gweneth serve juice, coffee, scrambled eggs, bacon, and toast.

"Did Santa stop by, Autumn?" Camryn asked.

"He left me lots of things," Autumn said.

"You can show me after breakfast," Camryn said.

The phone shrilled, and Marcus rose.

"Maybe it's Mum and Dad," Olivia said.

Marcus shrugged, his scowl grim. "I doubt it."

What kind of parent didn't want to spend a holiday with their children? Amme couldn't understand this, but kept her comments to herself.

He returned with the phone, grinning. "It's Max."

"Put it on speaker," Camryn said. "That way, we can all wish him a happy Christmas. Hi, Max. Merry Christmas!"

Everyone spoke at once, offering Christmas greetings, and Max's and Luke's voices burst into the room. Even Ellen said hello, and Amme was happy for Camryn because she knew her sister-in-law's attitude hurt.

That set the tone for the rest of the day. The sun shone hot, and the sky remained cloudless for most of the day. They played cricket, had a boisterous game of pool volleyball to cool down, and enjoyed their barbecue lunch and the salads and desserts they'd prepared together in the big kitchen.

"It must be present time now," Olivia said, rubbing her hands together once the dishes were done and the remnants of lunch cleared away. "I can't wait to see what my Secret Santa got me."

Gweneth jumped up and down in excitement. Amme fought a spurt of humor. Maybe her former charge wasn't as grown up as she thought. She'd never known this family atmosphere either and was blooming, no longer the timid child Amme had protected from her disappointed father.

"You do the honors, Olivia," Marcus said.

"Yay!" Olivia didn't waste any time and picked up the first present. "Nanu," she said and handed the present over.

"Should I wait or open it?" Nanu asked.

"Open," Autumn said, and everyone laughed.

He opened it to display a black rugby shirt and a rugby ball.

"That's the jersey for our national team," Marcus said.

"Cool," Nanu said and tugged his T-shirt off to exchange it for the rugby jersey. He beamed at everyone and did a twirl.

"Makeup," Gweneth squeaked, hugging an open vanity case to her chest. "Look, Amme. Just like Olivia's."

Amme admired the contents of the vanity, then turned her attention to Autumn, who was opening her parcel.

Autumn jumped up and down in the midst of a sea of colored wrapping paper and ribbons. "More books and a pink T-shirt. I like pink and blue."

Nanu whistled when Jannike held up a sexy piece of lingerie.

"Nice Secret Santa," Kaya said in admiration, her hands busy on her own parcel. "Yes, yes, yes! I have me some sexy lingerie too."

"Someone thinks I need more relaxation," Marcus said and held up a T-shirt and a book with a soldier on the front.

"They'd be right," Olivia said. "You work too hard."

"Not recently." Marcus gently tugged one of Autumn's pigtails. "I have someone important to spend my time with now."

"Me, Daddy?"

"Yes, you, pumpkin."

Her brow furrowed as she peered at Marcus. "I'm not a pumpkin. I'm a girl."

So sweet. Amme's gaze met Marcus's, and her sight picked the moment to start with the stupid prickling malady. She blinked rapidly, her lips stretching wide in a grin.

"There's one more present," Olivia said and picked up a big red-and-white-striped box. "It's for you, Marcus."

"Me? How come I get an extra one?"

"We wanted to get you something extra for allowing us to use your cottage and for your hospitality," Camryn said. "It's from all of us."

"Open it, Daddy," Autumn said.

Marcus removed the paper with quick efficiency. "A pétanque set!"

"What's pet tank, Daddy?"

"It's a game the French play. Like outdoor bowls. See this ball." He picked up a bright orange ball. "We divide into teams, and one team throws this ball. And then these balls." He showed a bigger one to Autumn. "We take turns throwing these and the winner is the team that gets their balls closest."

Autumn nodded, her pigtails bobbing. "Can you hit the other balls? Like crokay?"

Marcus grinned. "Yes, you can attack the other balls like we do in croquet."

"That sounds easy enough," Nanu said and winked at Kaya. "Cutthroat."

Jannike rubbed her hands together. "I like cutthroat."

"Excellent. I challenge everyone to a tournament," Marcus said. "Just as soon as we finish here. I have three more gifts to hand out for the ladies in my life." He strode out of the room and returned to hand a small box to Olivia, another to Autumn, and the final one to Amme.

Amme stared at him in surprise, her chest so tight she had to gasp for breath. Stupid heart-pump. She pressed a hand to her breast and massaged the offending area.

He brushed a kiss over her parted lips. "Open it, sweetheart."

With trembling fingers, she pulled back the tape and parted the paper to reveal a small box.

"Marcus, thank you," Olivia said. "I love it."

Autumn appeared beside them. "I want to wear now," she said, holding a glittering chain in her hand.

Amme opened the small box to find a golden chain with the letter A dangling off the end. Tiny sparkling jewels were embedded in the golden letter, making it glitter with white fire. "It's beautiful," she whispered.

"Look," Autumn said, and Amme saw a similar one in blush pink hanging around the little girl's neck.

Olivia already had her pendant hanging around her neck, the black onyx and gold in the shape of an O, perfectly suited to the girl's tastes.

"Thank you." Amme stood and wrapped her arms around Marcus. Cheers and smartass remarks rang out as she kissed him in front of his daughter, his sister, and her friends. She'd never been this happy in her living memory.

"This is the best Christmas day I've ever had," Olivia said when they had a quiet moment together while waiting for their turn to play pétanque.

Marcus nodded. "Even though the parents haven't rung?"

"Even though." She shrugged. "I don't have any expectations when it comes to Mum and Dad. I've learned it's easier that way."

"But it still damn well hurts. I hate to say it, but some people shouldn't have children."

Olivia shot him a look then, her expression much older than her years. "Do you regret Autumn?"

"Not in a million years. I love her."

"She's easy to love," Olivia said. "Did you want to be a dad?"

"I didn't ever plan on having kids. After Mum and Dad's example, I thought it was best not to saddle any kids with the same pattern of behavior."

"We're not our parents. I refuse to behave like them," Olivia said.

"We've made a satisfactory start," Marcus said, gesturing at the people around them.

Camryn and Amme were showing Autumn how to hold the ball and throw it toward the jack ball.

"Your turn, Olivia," Camryn called. "Make it a good one. Nanu is way too smug. We need to beat his arse."

Several hours later Marcus sipped from his can of beer and watched a competitive and slightly vicious game of croquet, but his mind kept circling around to the note he'd found on his office desk when he went to collect his camera. The note hadn't been there before. He was sure of it. Camryn or her friends weren't responsible, but he hated to think of Sophie invading his office, his house.

You'll be sorry.

Hell, he didn't even know if Sophie was responsible for the note, but if she was, how the hell had she managed to get the note into his office? During the past weeks, someone had always been around—except during their group outings.

But still, he locked up and set the alarm when they left the premises. Mostly. Perhaps he needed to take more care with security, especially now that Autumn was around.

"What's wrong?" Amme slid her arms around his waist, after returning from putting Autumn to bed. "You're scowling."

"Nothing. Just thinking." A lie, of course, and it didn't sit well, not when he was speaking to Amme. No, he was protecting her, Olivia and his daughter from a woman with bats in her mental attic.

"It's been a lovely day. Thank you for having us here and letting us celebrate Christmas. It...well, this means a lot to us."

"You're welcome, but you and your friends have made this day extra special for me and Olivia too. Our mother and father aren't exactly demonstrative. We've never had this sense of family."

"Really?" Amme curled her cool fingers around his in a gesture of comfort. "Their loss."

"I think so." For years, he'd thought he'd turned out just like his father, his mother. Now he wasn't so sure.

"Camryn and I are heading back to Max's," Ry said. "Camryn said we need to rest up if we wanted to hit the Boxing Day sales. I don't enjoy shopping."

"Me neither," Marcus said.

"The non-shoppers can always stay here and cook a meal for our return," Camryn said. "Besides, I thought you and Nanu wanted to do a few things."

"I can help," Marcus said. "Anything to avoid shopping."

"You're both scaredy cats," Camryn said with a tilt of her chin and laughter swimming in her expression.

Ry's brows rose, his full attention focused on Camryn. "Was that an insult? What's that saying you quote at me? Pot. Kettle."

Camryn patted his arm. "I'm going to buy a wedding dress. I don't require your presence anyway."

"You're getting married?" Marcus asked. "I thought you were already."

"We're mates," Ry said.

"Yes, but—"

Amme cut him off. "They wanted to renew their vows here with her family. On New Year's Day."

"Actually," Camryn said. "We meant to ask you if we could have the ceremony here. Your garden is gorgeous and just perfect for photos."

"A wedding?" Olivia butted in and clapped her hands once in

enthusiasm. "That's so exciting. I can't wait to go shopping now. I know some great dress stores."

"Thanks," Camryn said. "We can do with the inside knowledge. We're leaving early, though, to get the best bargains. No sleeping in."

Marcus laughed. "No late night for you, Olivia. You're grumpy if you miss out on your sleep."

"See you tomorrow," Camryn said with a wave and a wink.

"I'm tired myself," Amme said as Ry and Camryn strode to their vehicle. "Autumn was super juiced with the excitement. I might check she's sleeping and go to bed too. I'll see everyone for breakfast."

"Juiced?" Olivia asked.

"Um, over excited." Amme averted her gaze to stare at her feet.

"I'll come with you," Marcus said, and his mind wasn't on shopping at all. Nor was it on the odd expressions he kept hearing from Amme and her friends.

"Good night," Mogens said.

"Make sure you sleep," Kaya said and waggled her eyebrows.

"Adults," Amme said.

Olivia poked her fingers in her ears. "La, la, la."

A bark of amusement escaped Marcus, and he lifted a hand in farewell. "See you tomorrow morning."

He and Amme ascended the stairs together, stopping to check on his daughter before retiring.

The instant the door shut behind them, he took Amme in his arms. His mouth settled on hers, and he put every bit of emotion into the kiss, telling her of his thanks, his love, his intentions.

Clawing tension filled him, the need to touch and stroke her silken limbs. He backed her toward the bed and when she toppled, he followed her down, swallowing her eep of shock with his mouth. He laughed and laughed again when she hit him.

"That wasn't funny."

"I've never heard you make that sound before."

"And you won't hear me make it again, if I have anything to say about it," she muttered.

His lips brushed her ear then he laid a trail of kisses down her neck. He sucked and nipped, instantly soothing the sting of pain when Amme moaned and clutched him tighter.

"I need you naked. Want to suck on those luscious breasts of yours."

"Yes," she said. "The dress has a—"

"Back zipper. I did it up for you, remember?" He rolled off her and helped her to her feet, making quick work of undressing. Her apricot-colored sundress slipped down her body to reveal a matching apricot bra and panties. He stepped back to get a better view. "God, you are so sexy. I don't know where to touch first."

Amme reached behind to unfasten her bra. He watched, mesmerized by her soft curves and tawny skin.

"You're lagging behind," she said and stepped out of her panties.

He whisked off his clothes, scooped her up and placed her on the center of his bed. Perfect, he thought. Unable to resist, he kissed her again, soft and hard then soft again until her breathing turned harsh and the atmosphere cracked with sensual tension. His hands skimmed and caressed, touching every part of her sexy form.

"You make me crazy with want," he whispered as he slipped into her. He faltered an instant, realizing he'd forgotten a condom. To hell with it. He trusted her—it was that simple. He embedded himself as deep as he could go, wallowing in her heat and tightness, her sigh of acceptance.

"Take me hard, Marcus. I want to feel you inside." She arched her hips and plunged her fingers into his hair, holding him close.

His heart beat a sharp staccato against his ribs as he increased the pace of his thrusts. Her channel rippled around his dick, each hard, tormenting stroke driving him fast and powerfully toward completion. He stole another kiss, and when he lifted his head, her whiskey eyes were fogged with hunger. A potent thing. He plunged into her, each stroke rough and hot and raw.

A fine sheen of sweat coated his skin, and each thrust pushed him higher, the slide into her full of exquisite friction.

"Amme. Amme," he murmured, the fire and chills warring inside him starting to crash together, his orgasm a hairsbreadth from detonation. Gritting his teeth, he pulled out of her.

"What is it?"

"Turn over for me. Up on your hands and knees. Yeah, just like that," he said and entered her from behind, drove into her tight, grasping heat. In this position, he went deeper, and he had easy access to both her breasts and her clit. "You are so sexy. Amme, you turn me inside out."

She glanced over her shoulder, her gaze full of questions. "Inside out."

"You put me off balance. You've upset my usual unpredictable life." He surged into her again, his balls so damn tight they hurt. "That's a very good thing," he purred into her ear. "In case you're wondering."

"I'm glad." The momentary tension in her shoulders released, relaxed.

Her pussy clenched around his shaft, and his breathing caught. So close. So close. He reached beneath her to finger her clit and rubbed back and forth over the hard nub. A shudder vibrated through her limbs, and her sheath gripped his cock in hard uneven pulses.

"Come for me, sweetheart." He rubbed her clit again, and she moaned, the sound music to his ears. One last stroke had her shuddering, a signal he could seek his own release. He pulled back, his shaft coated with her juices, and slammed home, almost seeing stars as the tension inside him snapped and pleasure swamped his senses. The contractions of his cock went for a long time before stilling. Marcus nuzzled her neck, her skin fragrant with her sweet scent and a hint of his own musk.

Marcus pulled out of her and tugged her into his arms, the satisfaction welling inside him almost too much to contain.

Amme yawned, and Marcus laughed.

"You've tired me out."

"Go to sleep, sweetheart. You have a big day tomorrow."

Her breathing slowed, but Marcus took longer to drift off to sleep. Too many thoughts danced through his mind. Autumn. Olivia. Bloody Sophie. And Amme. He smiled at the woman curled so trustingly in his arms, his heart full, emotions leaning to tender. They'd just made love, yet he wanted her again.

He wanted her full stop.

The next few days passed in a flurry of activity. Shopping. Wedding plans. The New Year's Eve party. Costumes, since they'd decided to make the party fancy dress. But although Amme kept busy with these events plus looking after Autumn, the clock was steadily ticking down the moments until their departure.

The idea of leaving Autumn and Marcus made her heart-pump ache, and she didn't know what to do.

"Amme." Camryn snapped her fingers in front of her face. "I asked you what you thought of this dress."

It was plain and cream with a fitted beaded strapless bodice that took the gown from simple to stunning.

"You look beautiful. This dress is perfect. This is the one."

Camryn nodded. "I think so too. At last! I feel as if we've been shopping for days. Now a gown for you. Which color would you like?"

"Me?"

"Yes, you're going to be my bridesmaid. My special attendant.

Let me see." Camryn turned around and started going through the rack of dresses. "No. No. No." She pulled out a gown in a similar style to hers, the shade a close match to Amme's eyes. "This one. Try it on. Go. Go." She made a shooing motion with her hands.

Amme stood, wavered a fraction while her cybertronics behaved plain weird. Everything inside her leaped about then clenched—sort of like dancing an energetic jig before dropping into an exhausted heap. She pressed her hand to a spot between her breasts and rubbed to ease the turmoil. The entire time she stared at Camryn, the weird stinging malady striking again. The tingle smarted so much a drop of water leaked from one eye. She trapped it with her fingertip and stared at it in confusion.

She was crying. She never cried.

"What's wrong?" Camryn asked.

Amme shot a glance at the storeowner, who was still dancing attendance on another bride and her mother. She leaned closer to Camryn. "My body is malfunctioning, I tell you." She held out her wet finger. "I'm leaking water and my cybertronics, my heart-pump keeps jumping out of beat."

A slow smile spread across Camryn's lips, a mysterious smile, one that hinted at a juicy secret. "I know this isn't normal for cyborgs, but what you're describing sounds like emotions. How do you feel about being part of my wedding?"

"I'm excited and honored and...and..." Another tear rolled free.

"You're touched by my request." Camryn hugged her and the show of friendship sent her heart-pump jumping like a skipping-bean from the planet Greet. "You're experiencing emotions."

"I...me? I don't feel emotions. I'm designed to supervise children, to care and nurture them. That is all. I don't love them."

"Maybe not in the past. What would you do if someone attacked Gweneth?"

"I'd gut them."

Camryn nodded. "Yet according to you, your programming should only work for Autumn since you are now her minder."

"But—"

"And what if someone tried to hit me?"

"I'd try to protect you," Amme said without hesitation.

"And Marcus?"

"I'd stop them," Amme said with a ferociousness that took even her aback.

Camryn tapped a finger against her temple. "Emotions. Now go and try on that dress so we can meet the others at the mall."

Amme took the dress and walked into the changing room, her mind only half on the task. Emotions were impossible for her. Weren't they? She removed her denim skirt and her sleeveless cream shirt and took a moment to admire her lingerie. Her body didn't require lingerie, but she liked the lacy bits of nothing. They made her feel feminine. Human like Camryn. She shook her head at the thought. An abnormal notion and one that her fellow cyborgs would despise. They were a race who'd deleted their emotions in order to live good, solid and useful lives. Productive ones without the useless clutter of feelings and physical limitations.

Somehow, her mind and body had suffered a blip.

While she slid on the whiskey-colored dress, she did a quick internal self-check. Nothing appeared out of the ordinary.

"What's taking so long?" Camryn asked through the dressing room curtain. "Doesn't it fit?"

Amme tugged aside the curtain. "It's a perfect fit, but I need help with the zipper." She turned to present her back, and Camryn pulled up the zip.

Camryn clapped her hands together when Amme turned in her direction to display the strapless dress with the embroidered flowers on the bodice. "It's perfect. This is the one. Now on to the mall and shoes."

"I'm going to ask Amme to marry me." Marcus blurted the words to Olivia during a quiet moment with just the two of them.

"You what?"

"You resemble a fish. You'll catch a fly if you're not careful."

"Well, you took me by surprise," Olivia said and smacked him on the shoulder. "I thought you were a confirmed bachelor."

"I didn't think I had it in me to be a father either. Hell, look at our parents."

"I'd rather not," Olivia said. "They still don't know I'm here. As far as I know, they haven't tried to contact me." Her mouth twisted. "I don't think they'd miss me if I left Earth."

Marcus reached for her sister and gave her a quick hug. At first, she resisted, then she pressed against his chest, and he wrapped his arms around her, giving her the comfort she needed.

After a long moment, she pulled back. "Would you miss me?"

"Yes." Amme's presence had done more than help him with his daughter. She'd help him become closer to his rebel sister. "In fact, I was going to ask if you want to stay with me."

"And crash a couple of honeymooners?"

"The house is huge," Marcus said. "Say yes."

"But I need to do something," Olivia said. "I can't just mooch off you."

"So work out what you want to do and make this your base. You're my family, Liv. I want you here."

Olivia stared at him, then brought a shaky hand to her chin. "You haven't called me that for years."

"I know. I lost my way for a while. Amme has made me take a hard look at my life, and I didn't like what I saw. Slowly, day by day, I was turning into our parents."

"Yuck." Olivia wrinkled her nose. "A fate worse than death."

"So you'll stay?"

"Yes, for the time being anyway." She hesitated. "I've thought about doing something in travel. Not the same as Mum and Dad's business, but more adventure-related travel."

Marcus grinned. "Adventure like our ancestor, the great Marco Polo?"

"Yes."

"So do it. I'll help you in any way I can."

Olivia flew at him and wrapped her arms around him in a fierce hug. "Thank you."

"So I guess this means you're happy about Amme joining the family?"

"It's the best move you've ever made," Olivia said. "Amme is perfect for you. Don't you dare let her escape. When are you going to ask her?"

"I pick up the ring tomorrow. I need you to babysit Autumn tomorrow night so I can take Amme out for a special dinner."

"Done deal." Olivia rubbed her hands together. "I love Amme. I can't wait for her to join our family—the new, improved Polos."

CHAPTER NINE

"My feet are sore," Amme said.

"Mine too," Camryn said, stretching her bare feet out in front of her and wriggling her toes.

"I'm not surprised," Ry said. "I think you bought out the shops."

"It's a special occasion," Amme said. "I can't wait for the wedding."

Marcus lifted one of her feet and placed it on his lap. He rubbed her arches with gentle pressure, and a soft groan of pleasure rushed past her lips.

"Ooh, that's good. Don't stop," Amme said.

Camryn sighed. "We should go back to the cottage. I promised Max I'd help with the training in the morning. Early morning," she added. "I don't want to miss this since we're leaving soon."

Ry stood and pulled Camryn to her feet. "Let's go then. Are the others still out?"

"Olivia has taken them night clubbing. I doubt they'll be back for hours," Camryn said.

Marcus gave a theatrical shudder. "It's kind of scary knowing my sister is legal now. She got into enough mischief before she turned twenty. She got herself expelled from countless schools for sneaking into pubs."

Camryn laughed. "The way I hear it, daughters can be a lot of trouble. You have that to look forward to."

Marcus groaned. "Don't tell me that."

"I need to recharge," Amme said. "We have to start party prep tomorrow."

"It's not too late to hire a catering company," Marcus said. "We can find one somewhere willing to cater the party."

"No, we want to do this. It's our way of saying thank you for sharing your holiday and home with us," Camryn said.

Amme nodded. "With all of us helping it's fun, not work anyway."

"Good night," Ry said and urged his mate to the door. "We need to rest."

"Is rest a different word for sex?" Camryn asked.

"It's a word meaning bottom spanking," Ry said.

Marcus grinned and walked them to the door. "See you tomorrow."

Amme stood and went to check on Autumn. The little girl was just as exhausted as the rest of them. Her arm and leg stuck from beneath the covers, and Amme resettled the sheet. She looked cute and peaceful. Although she was a serious child, she'd blossomed under Marcus's attention. Amme smiled as she exited Autumn's room and broke into a little dance shimmy, which took her into Marcus's bedroom. She liked to think she'd helped too.

"Is Autumn asleep?" Marcus wrapped an arm around her waist and pressed a kiss to her temple.

"Yes, I think we tired her out today."

"I'll run a bath for you."

"You don't have to do that."

Marcus placed his lips on hers then took the contact deeper until their tongues tangled and excitement flared in a bright burst. She clung to him, gloried in the quivers of pleasure, of desire. The roam of his fingers. When their mouths parted, her lungs labored to catch a breath and Marcus seemed in the same condition.

"I love you, Amme. Go and grab whatever sexy lingerie you're going to torture me with tonight. I'll start the water running." He strode away and disappeared into his en suite, leaving her staring after him. Secs later the sound of water splashing into the tub drifted to her.

He loved her?

Amme blinked. Other people loved, spoke of their feelings. She was a childcare cyborg because she'd exhibited the trait in early childhood. Cybertronics enhanced her body to increase the characteristic.

Love wasn't meant for her.

She wasn't meant for love.

Yet, Marcus's words made her knees tremble, and she tottered to the drawers containing her lingerie to follow his instructions.

He loved her.

"The bath is ready," Marcus called, and the water shut off.

Amme hurriedly grabbed the first nightgown to hand. It didn't matter which one because she usually ended up naked anyway. Besides, the ability to think seemed to have packed up and gone on holiday.

She stepped into the bathroom and found Marcus stripping off. Soft music played from concealed speakers and several candles flickered, saving the room from full darkness and giving it an intimacy that increased the boom, boom, boom of her heart-pump. She halted, her gaze tracing his muscled chest, trim

145

waist, and strong thighs. Immediately, she went gooey inside.

Gooey.

It wasn't a word Amme had used or understood until she met Camryn. Evidently, Ry made Camryn go gooey, but Amme had never quite comprehended the feeling, not in the same way as her friend.

Now she did.

Marcus made her feel this way, and she liked it even if it meant she should seek a tune-up from Mogens.

"I thought we'd share," he said.

"I like the way you think." Boom, boom, boom. Was this love? *Grata*, she didn't know. All she knew was that the idea of leaving Marcus and Autumn made her eyes sting and her stomach churn. And her heart-pump...out of control.

"Let me undress you," he murmured, his breath warm against her ear. A tremor went through her, and she shivered again at the touch of his fingers against her ribs. When she was finally naked, he helped her step into the bath and turned on the jets. Soon Marcus settled into the bath behind her and drew her against his chest.

"You always smell good."

One of her cyborg traits, but she couldn't tell him that. "Thank you."

"I love spending time with you. These last few weeks have been amazing." Marcus paused to pump liquid soap into his palms. He ran his soapy hands over her shoulders and breasts, using seductive strokes that pushed at her desire.

She relaxed against him, her neck pillowed by his shoulder. "It's been special for me too. It's hard to believe it's almost time to leave."

"What if you didn't have to go? Would you want to stay?"

"Yes." She didn't even need to think about it, but secs later the problems, the differences between them pounced into her mind like a big cat. She bit her bottom lip and pushed away her fears.

Somehow...there might be a way. Her teeth dug deeper into her lip. Kuf! Who was she trying to fool?

Staying with Marcus would be like living a lie, and she wasn't sure how long she could keep up the pretense. What would happen if she malfunctioned?

Not that this happened on a regular basis, but malfunctioning was always a remote possibility.

Unaware of her inner turmoil, Marcus kept touching and stroking and caressing until she wriggled in his embrace.

"Well, we'll have to see if we can manage that." Marcus's hands slid over her breasts, and he kissed her neck. "We'll talk about a plan tomorrow because right now, I want to enjoy you." His hands slipped down her torso, over her hip and between her thighs. His finger stroked and delved, her flesh soft and hot and needy. Pleasure swirled through her. Not with an urgent tempo but something gentler and sweeter.

A plan? The thought pierced her foggy pleasure then dispersed like Martian mist.

The bubbles forced from the jets helped to soothe her aching muscles, and she floated in a blissful state. Marcus stroked her—*oh yes*—did some precision work on her clit, rubbing and teasing until the pleasure burst over her.

"Marcus," she whispered, her internal muscles moving in hard spasms for long moments. The press of his cock into her back reminded her this loving was very one-sided. She attempted to twist her body, but he held her in place.

"Don't worry about me," he said. "We have the rest of the night." He nibbled her neck, and her head fell back, exposing more flesh for his attentions.

"That feels so good." Her cybertronics jumped and gamboled like a playful puppy.

He teased one nipple, alternatively plucking and pinching until enjoyment radiated from each point of contact.

"We're turning into prunes," Marcus said.

An unfamiliar term. She opened her mouth then clamped it shut. It couldn't be life-threatening since there was no panic in his voice.

"We should get out before your beautiful skin goes permanently wrinkled. Out you get. I'll take care of things in here. You keep warm." Marcus gave her a gentle push and she rose to her feet and stepped from the bath.

She lifted her hand and saw her normal smooth skin, yet prunes related to wrinkling in some way. She made a mental note to ask Camryn about this phenomenon.

Marcus grabbed a handful of soap and washed himself briskly.

She stared for an instant, the towel she was drying herself with stilling. A cool shiver went over her, pebbling her skin with tiny chill bumps. She cocked her head, listening closely, frowned. She dropped the towel and smoothed on a black lacy gown.

"You look beautiful," Marcus whispered. "Don't get cold. Go and climb in bed."

His heated look warmed her through, and she nodded. "Don't be long."

"With you waiting for me? Not a chance."

Amme padded through to the bedroom, and another chill swept over her. Autumn. Something wasn't right. Instinct had her moving before the thoughts formed into solid commands to act. She burst into Autumn's room and discovered an empty bed.

"Autumn?"

"Amme!" Panic filled the child's voice.

Amme charged in the direction of the stairs. Three-quarters of the way down Autumn struggled with a strange woman. "What are you doing? Autumn, come to me."

"Stay away from me," the woman screeched, her eyes wild, her blonde hair unkempt. The chipped scarlet fingernails of her right hand dug into Autumn's upper arm. The blade of a knife glinted in the other. "Stay away or...or I'll hurt her."

The knife wavered in her trembling hand, and a bead of blood formed on Autumn's cheek.

Amme froze, her mind fumbling for English. "A-Autumn is an innocent. Please, please let her come to me."

"Get back!"

Amme summed up with cyberspeed. If she got close enough, she'd grab Autumn. Her strength and speed would aid her.

"Amme." Autumn wriggled. "I want Daddy."

"It's all right, sweetheart," Amme said, not taking her attention from the woman. "I've seen you before. In the mall. Have you been following us?"

"S-stay where you are. I'll use my knife. Cut her pretty face. Marcus won't want her anymore."

"Marcus loves her," Amme said. "He'd love her no matter what."

"Marcus loves me." The woman's voice wavered, and her gaze bounced from Amme to the landing above and back.

"What do you want?"

The woman cleared her throat, hesitated before bursting into speech. "M-Marcus is mine. Tell him I'm taking his daughter. He can come for her. W-we're gonna be happy. I love him."

Amme gathered herself. She could do this, move before the woman reacted.

Autumn snapped her teeth, diverting the woman's attention. Amme leaped, struck the woman's hand. The knife flew over the banister. But the woman reacted quickly. She shoved Autumn against the wall and sprang at Amme, fingers outstretched. Pain receptors registered the gouge, the damage to her chin.

"You can't have him," the woman snarled, and she grabbed Autumn and pushed her down the stairs.

"Autumn!" Amme shrieked.

Autumn screamed, legs and arms flailing as she toppled

backward. Amme practically flew after Autumn, grabbing her, using every bit of her strength to save the girl from harm.

She managed to grip the banister and halt their downward roll. She dug in, taking their combined weight on her legs. Exhaling a shaky breath, she set Autumn down, made sure the child had her balance.

Marcus appeared at the top of the stairs. "What the fuck? Sophie?"

"She can't have you," the woman shrieked, and she jostled Amme, elbowed her, then rammed her hard.

Amme went airborne. She tumbled backward and hit the bottom stair with a thump that reverberated inside her skull.

Pain struck her like a blow—a blast of agony doubled by her receptors and echoing through her blood network. Move. She had to move. A groan escaped as she ordered her body to move. Her leg. *Grata*, her leg. It bent at an impossible angle. She gasped, tried to propel herself forward with her arms. Her right arm crumpled, and she realized she was broken.

Summoning every bit of energy, she forced her head to move and glanced at her arm. The skin covering her arm circuitry had split and some of her cybertronics were visible.

Panic roared through her mind, her thoughts tangling as she attempted to pick herself up again.

Camryn. Camryn would help. She had to...to com Camryn.

"Amme," Marcus shouted.

Amme managed to croak a garbled message via her earpiece before blackness clouded her mind. "Emergency. Code blue. Code blue!"

Marcus shoved past Sophie, ignoring her shrieks to get to Autumn and Amme.

"Marcus, I love you," Sophie sobbed.

"Get the fuck out of my way." He reached Autumn, her small

face pale and tear-streaked, a little bloody. The red brushed away with his thumb. Superficial. Thank God. "Autumn, are you all right? Do you hurt anywhere?"

"She...she...is Amme dead like Mummy?"

"No, of course not." He picked up Autumn and continued down the stairs, hoping like hell he wasn't lying to his daughter. "Stand over there, sweetheart, while I check Amme."

"Marcus, you're mine," Sophie screamed. She wrapped her arms around herself and curled into a weeping ball on the landing. "It's not fair. You belong to me."

He ignored her to crouch beside Amme. Her eyes were wide open, blank, and staring. Grief and pain struck him as he fumbled to check her pulse. His fingers touched cool, clammy skin at her throat.

No pulse.

He reached for her wrist and— "What the fuck?" Those were wires. Some kind of circuits. "Autumn, I want you to run and get my phone. It's on the kitchen counter."

Without warning, a window smashed. Marcus whirled in time to see a huge black leopard leap into his house. Seconds later, another one followed. Marcus blinked and blinked again when the biggest leopard suddenly morphed into a man.

Ry.

The second leopard transformed into a topless Camryn. Ry let out a snarl, and Camryn immediately crossed her arms over her bare breasts.

"Is she all right?" Camryn demanded. "What happened? Where's Autumn?" She paused to listen. "The others are almost here."

"What the fuck?" Marcus said. "You...you..."

"Broken arm. Broken leg. Must be shock. She's gone offline. We need Mogens and Nanu," Ry said in a terse voice. "Shut up," he snarled at Sophie.

"Daddy, here's the phone," Autumn said. "Where are your clothes?"

"I was in a hurry," Camryn said. "Marcus, what happened?"

"I don't know. I was in the bathroom. I heard a scream and came out in time to see Amme hit the ground."

"The lady tried to steal me," Autumn said.

"Look after your daughter," Ry ordered. "We'll take care of Amme."

"What do you mean she's offline? I couldn't find a pulse." Anguish wrapped around him. Shock. He shook his head, trying to reorder his thoughts. "I couldn't find a pulse. I think she's dead."

His front door flew open, Jannike and Kaya leading the rush, weapons in hand, their faces hard and determined.

"Amme!" Gweneth cried.

"Gweneth." Camryn grabbed her before she could reach Amme. "We think she's okay. I need you to find me a T-shirt. Can you do that?"

"Yes," Gweneth said. "You promise she's all right?"

"I think so. Mogens will tell us."

"Where is Mogens?" Ry demanded.

Marcus sank onto the floor, fear and disbelief stealing his ability to stand. Autumn went to him, pressed against him, and he wrapped his arms around her quivering body.

"Mogens stopped to get his satchel," Nanu said. "Kuf! I can see her circuitry. Kaya, I need my kit too."

"On it," Kaya said.

Olivia sidled up to him, her features pale as she dropped onto the floor beside him. "What the fuck is going on? We were dancing in the nightclub, having fun, then all of a sudden, they sprinted from the club. They were muttering code blue." Olivia paused to smooth some hair from her cheek. "I have never traveled so fast in all my life. Jannike...my god! I can't believe we made it here in one piece. Marcus, they aren't speaking English. I think...I think they're aliens," she finished in a whisper.

"Shut her up," Ry said. "She's getting on my nerves."

"On it," Jannike said and stalked up the stairs. She yanked Sophie to her feet and manhandled her to the ground floor. Jannike came to a halt beside Marcus. "What do you want me to do with her?"

"I'll call the cops. Look after Autumn for me," he said to Olivia.

"We'll take Amme back to the cottage," Ry said. "Mogens, will that work?"

"Yes, I can fix her."

Ry picked up Amme and strode to the front door.

"Wait, you can't just take Amme," Marcus objected.

"You can't help her," Ry said.

"Marcus, call the cops," Camryn said, and she darted after her friends, leaving Marcus alone with his sister and daughter and a sobbing Sophie.

Autumn patted his bare leg, and he realized he was naked apart from his boxer-briefs. "Will they make Amme better?" she asked.

"I hope so," he said.

He picked up his phone and dialed 1-1-1, the emergency number, and spoke to the dispatcher in a hard voice. He hung up. "The police are on their way."

"You understood them," Olivia said. "Autumn understands them too. How is that possible? All I could hear was clicks, interspersed with snaps and snarls. They really are aliens."

"We'll discuss it later," Marcus said. Right now, he was having trouble wrapping his brain around Ry and Camryn. He'd heard Amme mumble something before he reached her but hadn't realized she'd called for help.

"I wonder if Max knows," Olivia said.

"We'll discuss it later," Marcus reiterated in a hard voice.

Sirens sounded in the distance, quickly becoming louder.

"Cops are here. Let me do the talking."

"It's not fair," Sophie sobbed. "You're mine."

Marcus sent her a disgusted look and marched to the door. "In here, officers."

"What's the problem?" one of the policemen asked.

"This woman entered my home uninvited and tried to kidnap my daughter."

"Do you know who she is?"

"An ex-girlfriend. I broke it off some time ago, but she refuses to take no for an answer. I want her charged."

One of the policemen went to Sophie and helped her to her feet. "He belongs to me. He's mine. Mine!" she shrieked. "You ask him. He'll tell you. He belongs to me, not that other woman."

"What other woman?"

Marcus shrugged. "I have no idea what she's talking about. She's obviously unbalanced."

Marcus patiently answered their questions, and finally, they left, taking Sophie with them. When the door shut behind them, Marcus started to clean up the glass and found materials to board up the window while Olivia put Autumn back to bed. He was just finishing when Olivia came down the stairs.

"How is Autumn? No, don't tell me. I'll go and see for myself." He strode up the stairs, only slowing when he entered her room.

He found her curled in a ball beneath the covers, the night light glowing. Her breaths were slow and even, indicating she'd fallen asleep, despite the traumatic evening. He crouched beside the bed and resettled the covers over her slight form. Thank god she wasn't injured.

If Amme hadn't been there...

He shuddered and stood, leaving Autumn's bedroom door open so he'd hear her if she woke in distress.

"You want a cup of tea?" Olivia asked.

"I need something stronger." Marcus stalked to the pantry

and retrieved a bottle of whiskey. He found two glasses and poured a healthy measure into each one. "Hell of a night." An understatement.

His mind kept shying from the vision of Amme lying at the bottom of the stairs.

"They're aliens, I tell you," Olivia said.

"Do you know Camryn's cell phone number?"

"It's on the bit of paper stuck to the fridge. Amme wrote it down for me the other day since she doesn't have a phone."

Marcus gulped down some whiskey and stood. He retrieved the number and dialed, his stomach bucking and hollowing while he waited for Camryn to answer.

"Yes." Camryn sounded impatient.

"It's Marcus. How is Amme?"

"She's conscious now."

"Is she going to be all right?"

"I think so," Camryn said.

"Shouldn't she go to a hospital?" He asked the question, knowing what Camryn's answer would be.

"I don't think that's a good idea," Camryn said carefully. "What happened to the woman?"

"She's in police custody. The consensus is she's mentally unstable, and they're going to get a psychiatric report. She told the police there were strange people and big cats, and she thought they were aliens."

"I see," Camryn said after a pause. "What did you tell the police?"

"That she was stalking me, and it was a case of breaking and entering and attempted kidnapping."

"You knew about her?" The sharp note from Camryn brought a wave of guilt.

"She's been ringing and emailing me, but not to the point where I thought she was dangerous."

"Jannike said she's seen her around when we visited the mall."

"God." Marcus's hand tightened around the phone. "I didn't know."

"No one is blaming you, Marcus."

"I blame myself. I should've known she was unstable." He paused, took a gulp of his drink, enjoying the burn as it slipped down his throat. "Can I come and see Amme?"

Camryn hesitated. "She doesn't want to see you."

"Why? None of this is her fault. I don't blame her."

"I know. Ring me again tomorrow. She might change her mind." Camryn hung up abruptly, leaving him listening to dead air.

"How is Amme?" Olivia asked.

"She's awake but doesn't want to see me."

"She's had a shock," Olivia said. "Give her time. The party is in two days, then there's the wedding. Do you think they'll cancel?"

"Not if I have anything to do with it," Marcus said.

Olivia took a sip of her drink. "They're aliens, Marcus."

Marcus sucked in a deep breath, drank more. "Well, they're not human, but you know what. It doesn't matter a damn. I've never been so happy. Amme has made us into a family, and I'm not about to let that go."

"But they're leaving the day after the wedding."

"Amme's not leaving with them. I love her, and I'm not willing to let the best thing—the only woman I've ever loved—get away without a fight."

CHAPTER TEN

"Amme, sweetheart," Nanu said. "Please stop crying. The water will hurt your cybertronics." He frowned and shot her an enquiring glance. "I didn't think cyborgs could cry."

"I'm not meant to."

"Amme's body seems to have adapted and modernized itself," Mogens said. "Not a bad thing, but certainly unexpected."

"Are you sure Autumn is all right?" Amme asked for the third time.

Camryn wandered into the cottage bedroom where Mogens and Nanu were fixing Amme's broken arm and leg. "Marcus rang."

"Did you tell him I didn't want to see him?"

"Yes," Camryn said. "But I don't understand why."

"He deserves a woman who is whole, one who can give him more children, and I can't because of my childcare designation. Only those with parent designation can produce children on Sheng. I thought I'd told you that. Marcus deserves a human woman, one who can give him children."

"Rubbish," Camryn said. "You love him."

A tear rolled down Amme's cheek. "I'm a childcare cyborg, and that's all I'll ever be."

"You talk a load of crap," Camryn shot back. "You are the most caring person I know. Gweneth is a credit to you, and you're a valued member of our crew. But you deserve personal happiness, Amme. You want Marcus, and I think he wants you."

"There," Mogens said. "Test your arm."

Amme lifted her arm and it functioned as normal. It didn't look natural, though, with the workings showing through the jagged hole in her skin.

"Good. We'll place some healing gel on the wound and bandage it. I think the gel will promote new skin growth. At least that's what the healer said when I purchased it at the Intergalactic market on Shrimpton."

"I am lucky you're a skilled forecaster and predicted the need for the gel," Amme said. "This is the first time I've ever injured myself."

"Hopefully, it won't happen again," Mogens said. "But make sure you pay attention to how we fix you. You never know when you'll need to mend your own injuries."

Camryn yawned widely. "It's late. Do you need me for anything, or can I go to sleep?"

"Go and recharge," Nanu said. "Mogens and I are almost done with Amme's leg. Do you think it will be all right if we go back to the guest quarters at Marcus's place?"

Amme watched Camryn frown.

"I think so," she said finally. "We need to know what he's going to do now that he knows there is something weird about us. Set the perimeter alarms to give yourself warning if strangers come around."

"Will do," Nanu said. "Jannike and Kaya have already placed alarms. We didn't bother setting them tonight since we were all out. There, all done."

"See you in the morning, Amme. And don't worry. I'm sure everything will work out fine," Camryn said, and with a wave, she left the room.

Mogens applied gel to the patch and dressed it with a medicated bandage. "You'll need to recharge for the rest of the night. You can put weight on your leg in the morning. Com me if you suffer any unexplained pain."

"Thank you," Amme said.

"You're welcome, child," Mogens said.

Left alone, Amme recalled the expression on Marcus's face secs before her system shut down. Horror had marched across his features. Shock.

No, her friends were wrong. How could everything be all right after this?

"What are we going to do?" Camryn asked, her gaze roving over her mate's naked body. Despite the circumstances, it was difficult not to gawk at all that gorgeousness. And her mate would soon be her husband. The thought brought satisfaction and excitement. Peace.

Ry sprawled back in the bed, the sheet pooled over his groin. "Normally, I'd say we should leave, but this time is different. We want to come back to visit your family. We need to speak with Marcus and make sure he's willing to keep our secret."

"Olivia, too," Camryn reminded him.

"She'll be easier. We could intimidate her, put the fear of godly terror into her. Marcus is stronger, confident. His own man. He will do what he thinks is best, no matter how we apply threats."

"I'm sorry," Camryn said, laying her hand on his arm.

"You have no need to apologize. We discussed the risks before we came and tried to minimize them. I promised you we'd visit your family, and I'm not sorry. These weeks have been good for all of us."

Relief struck at the heart of Camryn, and she moved closer to kiss Ry.

"We'll go and speak with Marcus, try to gauge his attitude, and take things from there. We should go soon."

"I wish this hadn't happened before the party tonight. Everyone has worked so hard getting ready. Marcus will probably want to cancel," Camryn said.

"We'll ask, but no matter what, we're getting married tomorrow. I want to see you in your special dress."

"Good, because I would've dragged you up our makeshift garden aisle."

"That would make an excellent wedding photo. We could frame it and place it in our cabin on the Indy."

"Very funny, Cat Man."

"I thought so. We should visit Marcus now. Nanu and I are going to the Indy later to do our final maintenance checks. The repairs went surprisingly well. We were even able to stock up on parts we can adapt for use on the *Indy*. The junkyard Max told us about was a treasure trove."

"Good. Can you take my chair and find a place for it?"

"It's old."

"It's comfortable."

"It belonged to your husband."

"And then it belonged to me. You are my mate, and soon, you'll be my husband. I want the chair because it reminds me about how far I've come in the last year." Camryn climbed out of bed and stretched. "I suppose we should get this done so we know exactly where we are with Marcus. What? What's wrong?" she asked when Ry didn't move.

"You are beautiful, Camryn. Kidnapping you was the best thing I've ever done."

She grinned and leaped onto the bed, throwing herself at him. "Maybe we have time to say a proper good morning."

Their lips met, their hands became busy, and they didn't surface for another hour.

Amme tested her limbs and found they were working in the normal method. Apart from the bandages, she looked and felt like her usual self. The pipes in the walls banged when either Camryn or Ry turned on the shower. Such a different sensation from the sanitizers they used on the Indy. A shower with real water was one of the many things she'd miss when they left.

Amme climbed out of bed and realized she didn't have any clothes. She found a baby-blue robe on the back of the door and wrapped that around her waist before she wandered from her bedroom to find the kitchen. Camryn would have coffee. Sure enough, she found beans and filters, and she soon had coffee underway.

Ry entered the kitchen first. "How are you doing?"

"Almost as good as new. I'm sorry I've caused trouble."

"Not your fault." Ry drew her into a quick hug. "You were protecting a child. Camryn said she has some clothes you can wear."

"Thanks."

"We're going to see Marcus," Ry said.

"I want to come with you."

"I thought you never wanted to see him again," Camryn said,

appearing behind Ry.

"I've changed my mind. Hiding is cowardly, and I would come to regret not seeing Marcus one final time."

Ry nodded. "We'll wait for you to change."

"You have time to shower if you want," Camryn said.

"I need to check with Mogens about the bandages first. I don't wish for water damage."

Half an hour later, they strode out to speak to Marcus.

"I'm nervous," Amme said, the tremor in her hand highlighting her nerves.

Ry squeezed her arm, showing her that yet again, despite being alone, she'd ended up with a supportive family. "It will be all right. I've commed the others. They'll be on standby if we need them."

Camryn strode before them and thumped on the front door.

As they waited for someone to answer, Amme's stomach seemed to swirl—another anomaly in a string of many.

Mogens hadn't seemed concerned but she couldn't help but worry about the changes—the emotions and physical reactions that shouldn't appear yet kept occurring.

The door opened, and they were face-to-face with Marcus.

His haunted gaze went straight to her. "Amme." He pushed past Ry and Camryn and hauled her into his arms before she could speak.

At first, she held herself stiffly, unsure of how to react. Marcus trembled, his eyes closed as he held her. He was so big and strong and confident. That he would react in such a manner took her by surprise. Gradually, she relaxed into his embrace.

"We should go inside," Ry said in a low voice. "We need to talk."

Marcus pulled back, but he took her hand as if he were afraid to lose contact. "Of course. You're all right. I can't believe you're okay after your fall."

He led the way into the kitchen, the scent of coffee fragrant and enticing. Amme pulled out three more mugs and poured coffee for them all as well as topping up Marcus's cup.

Footsteps heralded an arrival. Olivia and Autumn.

"Amme, Amme, Amme," Autumn cried and flew at Amme. She flung her arms around Amme's legs and hugged her tight.

"Careful, Autumn. Don't hurt Amme's leg. It's still sore after last night," Marcus said.

Autumn frowned. "The lady pushed us down the stairs."

"She did," Amme said.

"Olivia said the police are growling at her now," Autumn said.

"That's right," Marcus said.

"We need to talk," Ry said. "But not in front of the child."

Marcus nodded. "Olivia, can you—"

"No," Camryn interrupted. "Olivia needs to hear this too. I'll com Gweneth to keep an eye on her. Is that acceptable to you?"

There was a moment of tense silence before Marcus nodded.

Camryn openly commed Gweneth, and a few mins later, she arrived along with the rest of the crew.

Amme tensed, wondering if Marcus would take this as a silent threat. The crew ganging up against him and Olivia. Her breath caught and slowly released when Marcus walked to her side and picked up her hand. His fingers closed around hers in silent reassurance.

"Help yourself to coffee," he said. "You might need to put on another pot." He lifted their linked hands and placed a kiss on her knuckles. "Are you really all right?"

"I will be. I need to recharge more."

Ry cleared his throat. "I am Ryman Coppersmith, from the planet Ibrox, but born on Viros, which is where we're going once we leave Earth. Amme and the others are part of my crew."

"I knew it!" Olivia said. "I knew there was something funny about these guys. What is he saying? I understand Amme easily, but some of the others don't seem as good at English."

"I have another translator," Mogens said. "Do I have your

permission to place it on your sister?"

"Do I already have one?" Marcus asked.

"It's a small thing, the size of a dot. I stuck one behind your ear several weeks ago. Autumn has one too." Amme watched his expression closely for any sign of distaste or horror. It didn't come.

"Go ahead," he said.

"What's happening?" Olivia demanded.

"Mogens is going to put a translator on you," Marcus said.

"Will it hurt?"

"Yes," he said.

"Marcus! It will not hurt," Amme said in English.

"Bring it," Olivia said with a cheerful grin. Her chin lifted to highlight the attitude. "How does it work?"

"It creates a pathway to the part of the brain that understands and interprets languages. You'll be able to understand any language," Mogens said after patting on the small patch.

"That could come in handy," Olivia said.

"The patch is much better than the red caterpillars they shoved into my ears," Camryn said with a shudder.

"You were a big baby-child," Kaya said. "Anyone would have thought we intended to kill you."

"No, you just kidnapped me instead," Camryn said sweetly.

"You're getting away from the point," Ry said with a glance at Marcus. "We came to Earth so Camryn could visit her brother. She had things she needed to say to him to explain her disappearance. We intend to leave on the second of January, and we'd appreciate it if you don't mention our existence to anyone else. We'd like to visit again in the future, and we can't do that if our presence puts Camryn's family in danger."

The entire time Ry spoke, Amme watched Marcus, her heart-pump beating faster than it should, nervous tension forcing her to swallow and swallow again. She waited for him to show disgust, to shove her away but it didn't happen.

Marcus frowned and glanced from Ry to Camryn and back. "I don't understand. You transformed from a leopard into a person. Both of you, but Camryn is Max's sister."

"I'm a leopard shifter," Ry said. "When Camryn and I became close, we mated and that changed her physiology."

"Cool," Olivia said.

"Quiet, Olivia," Marcus said. "Does Max know?"

"Yes," Camryn said.

"And Ellen?"

Camryn nodded.

"Okay." Marcus turned to Amme. "Tell me about you."

Amme swallowed, not enjoying becoming the center of attention.

"Amme, do you want me to tell Marcus?" Ry asked.

"No," she croaked. "I'll do it." She sucked in a breath in an effort to center herself. This was much harder than she'd anticipated. "I..." She sneaked a glance at Marcus, and her stomach started churning again. "I am from the cyborg race. Medical staff screen us as younglings and assign the roles our personality tests show will suit us. Our bodies are enhanced with technology to help us with our roles in order to make our society productive. I am a childcare cyborg." She stopped talking, unsure of how much she should say.

Camryn gave her a nod of encouragement, but no one else spoke. The pause lengthened until it became uncomfortable. Just as she was about to fill the gap, Marcus spoke.

"Is that why you became involved with me? Because I have a child?"

"No! I gravitate toward children, but I've never become involved with a parent before. I'm sorry I wasn't honest with you, but it was safer for all of us to remain incognito."

"We're going to leave you alone now, Amme. Is that all right?" Ry asked.

"Yes."

"We'll be outside in the garden. Com if you need us."

"But I want to listen," Olivia said. "I have questions."

"Out," Camryn said.

Olivia was still protesting when Camryn forcibly led her from the kitchen. "But Amme went swimming," she said. "Why doesn't she get rusty? Will you show me the changing thing? That's so radical. What about the others? What can they do? Ooh, how did you get here? Where's your space ship?"

"Good luck with finding her off button," Marcus said.

Amme heard Camryn chuckle as Olivia started another series of questions.

Amme waited, but when Marcus didn't say anything else, nerves made her plunge into the void. "Do I disgust you?"

"No! Of course not." Marcus turned her to face him. "Tell me about cyborgs."

"My race lives on the planet Sheng. The people of my planet value hard work and like to maximize profit. They believe that every citizen should be useful and specialization is the key to make this happen."

"So you became a childcare worker."

"Yes. I started work early, as soon as I graduated from formal training. Childcare cyborgs like me aren't expected to produce offspring. Any relationships are of a temporary nature because of my inbuilt need to nurture other people's children. I told you I can't have children. This is why. The ability to reproduce was adjusted when I was given enhancements."

He blinked at this, opened his mouth then shut it again. "How did you come to leave Sheng?"

"The older childcare cyborgs are given off-planet assignments. A portion of our wages goes back to our planet. Or it did. Once I left Ornum, which is where I met Camryn and Ry, my current contract was terminated. The controllers on Sheng will have marked me absent from duty. If I return to Sheng, they will

166

punish me."

"How?"

"Termination. My life has changed a lot since joining Ry and his crew. I have independence and friends."

"Hell." Marcus raked a hand through his hair, leaving a tuff standing on end. "I intended to ask you to stay when your friends left. I wanted to ask you to marry me." He searched her expression and sighed.

Euphoria grabbed her gut and twisted it then she noticed his expression, and her stomach plummeted. He'd wanted to ask her, not he intended to ask her. "But?"

"But now I don't know," Marcus said. "I need time to think."

"Do you want us all to leave right now?" Amme asked, and she was proud of her even tone. "Should we cancel the party?"

"Yes. No." He laughed, but it emerged strained and faded quickly. "You're only here for a few more days. It's too late to cancel the party, and besides, I'm not sure what excuse I'd give. No, we'll still have the party."

Amme tugged her hands from his. That was it then. "I'll...um...I'll go and tell the others."

For a sec, she thought he might stop her, might call after her and say he'd reconsidered. It didn't happen, and she walked outside into the sunshine, her mind charging in hundreds of different directions, her heart-pump galloping way too fast again.

Camryn saw her first and rushed to her side. "What is it? Tell me."

"He was going to ask me to stay, to marry him." Amme felt the prickling behind her eyes and knew she was about to cry. "I think he's changed his mind."

"What about the party?" Kaya asked, coming to join them.

"He said it's too late to cancel. The party will go ahead. He said it's all right for us all to stay until we leave."

"The wedding?" Camryn asked.

"I didn't ask, but I presume that is okay too." Amme shrugged and blinked rapidly. She forced a curve to lips that didn't want to crack a smile. "I'll go and pack."

"What the devil are you doing?" Olivia demanded. She tugged on Marcus's sleeve when he didn't answer. "You can't let Amme leave. She's upstairs packing."

Marcus brushed past Olivia and strode inside. She couldn't leave. That wasn't what he wanted. He took the stairs two at a time and barged into the room allocated to Amme.

She swiveled on his entrance, a pale apricot frothy bit of nothing clutched in her hand.

"You don't have to leave."

Amme turned away and dropped the piece of lingerie into an open case. "You don't want me here."

"I didn't say that. Amme!" Marcus grabbed her arm and held it until she gave him her attention. "I'm confused. I don't know what I think. Please stay here. Autumn won't understand if you move out. I don't want her to think it's her fault."

"I'm leaving anyway."

Marcus sighed. "I know. Autumn will think it's something she's done because you're living somewhere else. Coming so soon after her mother dying... I don't want her to think this is her fault." He slid a quick glance in Amme's direction and wasn't sure if she bought his reasons for her staying. The truth was he didn't know what to do, what to think, how to behave.

Amme was an alien.

He'd slept with an alien.

Hell, he was in love with an alien.

And didn't that beat all.

"Please stay for Autumn's sake. I won't make things difficult for you."

"How do I know I can trust you? What's to stop you from

causing trouble for me? Selling out my friends?"

"I'd do that if I thought you were putting Autumn at risk, and that's not the case. You put yourself in danger to save Autumn. When I asked Autumn what happened, she said the lady tried to push her down the stairs, and you stopped her. You broke Autumn's fall, which is the reason she's not in a hospital or worse right now. For that reason alone, I'd never do anything to put you or your friends in danger."

"Why should I...we trust you?"

"For the same reason, I trust you. Neither of us has done anything to warrant distrust," Marcus said. "I want you to stay, but the final decision is yours. If you feel more comfortable staying with Camryn or with your other friends, that's fine." Marcus stomped from the room. He found Camryn hovered at the base of the stairs.

"Everything all right?"

"I hope I've talked Amme into staying," he said.

"For good? Oh, that's great. I'm so pleased for you both."

"Until you leave." Marcus ignored the shock, the disappointment, evidenced by the slump of her shoulders. "Do you need anything else for the party?"

"No, everything is in hand."

"Good, I need to go out. Can you keep an eye on Autumn?"

"Sure," Camryn said. "At least you trust us to watch your daughter and not to hurt your sister." She shot him a glare and stalked off to join her friends. When she reached them, she spoke rapidly, and every one of them turned to glower at him, including his sister.

He opened his mouth to say something and closed it again because nothing he could say would make this better, not until he understood exactly what it was he thought. The implications, because it wasn't just himself to think about now. He had responsibilities. A daughter. His sister.

"Fuck," he muttered.

Marcus stalked inside, grabbed his car keys and his wallet, and a few minutes later, he screeched from the driveway, fishtailing on the loose gravel at the end of the drive. The car sped to the right from habit, yet he had no idea where he should go. The glimpse of the sign for Max's training stables decided him, and he slammed on the brakes, skidding a little as he made the turn.

Childish but satisfying.

He drove at a slower pace down the winding road to get to Max's house. Once there, he knocked on the door.

"Hi, Ellen," he said when she answered, her stomach bulging so much it appeared as if she could pop at any second. "I need to talk to Max. Is he around?"

"He's with clients down at the stables," she said. "Why don't you wait—"

But Marcus was already striding toward the stable block, his mind clearing from the fog currently shrouding his thought processes. He'd talk to Max. At least Max would understand what he was going through.

When he arrived at the stables he found Max speaking to four men while an assistant led a glossy chestnut thoroughbred around the yard. They wore designer suits but their shiny shoes had picked up dust during the tramp through the stables.

"The filly has excellent breeding and conformation. Early signs are good. She loves racing and hates another horse beating her." Max wore his boots, but his jeans and shirt appeared tidier than usual.

"Can we see her run?" one of the men asked.

"Sure." Max turned and noticed him lurking in the background. "Gentlemen, this is my neighbor, Marcus Polo."

"Ah, of the famous travel company," one said.

"My parents," Marcus said smoothly, the angst bucking like a grouchy horse in his gut subsiding with a slide into more normal channels. A familiar and comforting world, while the alien one he'd found himself thrust into just plain caused confusion.

"Did you need something?" Max asked.

"I wanted to speak with you, but it can wait. I'd love to see this horse run." He winked at the men. "Never know when I might want to add to my stable."

Max gaped at him.

"We have first refusal of this horse," one of the men said.

"Of course you do," Marcus said easily. "But I like what I see. She'd make a good purchase if she runs as good as she looks. That's if you decide not to take her. You don't mind if I watch her run too?"

"Of course not," the tallest of the men said, but Marcus caught the quick exchange of glances between the group.

Marcus slipped a sly wink at Max, and his friend grinned.

An hour later, Marcus stood beside Max and watched the men leave.

"They didn't even dicker about the price," Max said. "I'd priced her higher than normal because I knew they'd want a discount. You don't know anything about horses. You haven't been on a horse since you fell off when you were four. That's what you told me."

"Partly true. Amme and I took Autumn riding before Christmas. Brought all the bad memories back, but that doesn't mean I don't appreciate a fine beast." The thought led him directly to the reason he'd come here. "Your sister is a leopard shifter."

Max paled. "You can't report her to the authorities. They'd try to lock her up, her friends. Marcus, I'm begging you. Camryn is my sister."

"So you did know. They said you knew, but I wanted confirmation. Relax, Max. I'm not going to put Camryn or her friends in danger, especially when they've never done anything to warrant it. Besides, the authorities wouldn't believe me. If I wanted to cause trouble for your sister and her friends, I'd leak photos and info to the alien conspiracy theorists. They'd cause a ruckus."

"Hell." Max flinched, his shoulders stiffening. "Don't do that."

Marcus barked out a laugh. "Not gonna happen. You hear about my intruder?"

"Yeah, Camryn told me. You might as well come inside. I could do with a cup of coffee. Ellen will want to know what happened with the sale. This is the first of the horses I've bred for sale, and thanks to you, we got a great price."

Inside, with a coffee in front of him, he didn't know how to begin.

Blunt and straightforward, he decided. Get it out. "I've been sleeping with Amme. I'd decided to ask her to stay. I'd intended to ask her to marry me."

"But she's an alien," Ellen said.

"I didn't know that," Marcus said. "All I knew was a caring and beautiful woman who helped make me feel as if I could really be part of a family. She helped with Autumn and gave me confidence. And Olivia. Because of Amme, Olivia and I have reconnected."

"You didn't notice any differences?" Max asked.

"Not a one. When we first met, I heard them speak with strange clicks and grunts, but I thought they'd been mucking around. They all speak perfect English."

"They put a translator on you," Ellen said.

"Yeah. One on Autumn too. Although Amme's English has improved a lot. She can easily hold her own without a translator."

"Exactly how did you find out?" Max asked. "Camryn didn't have time to give me full details."

"I went out with a woman named Sophie a couple of times and broke it off because we didn't seem to mesh well. But she kept ringing and emailing me. I thought if I ignored it she'd finally go away, but things escalated. As far as I can make out, she managed to copy my house keys and let herself in. Her plan was to take Autumn, but Amme discovered her before she whisked Autumn away. The bitch pushed Autumn down the stairs. Amme—Amme managed to save her but ended up getting hurt." Marcus swallowed as the memories rushed through him. "When I reached her, Amme didn't have a pulse. Her leg twisted at a weird angle, and one arm... Her skin had torn, and I could see her circuitry."

"She's a robot?" Ellen asked.

"No, a cyborg," Max said.

"You knew?" Ellen demanded.

"Camryn is my sister. She told me everything," Max said. "Ellen, you didn't want to know, so I didn't tell you."

"You don't approve?" Marcus asked Ellen.

"You have to understand that Camryn put Max through hell before she disappeared. Then, we didn't know where she'd gone or what had happened to her. When she reappeared, I thought she'd just hurt Max again. I haven't spent much time with her friends, but Max and Luke have. I have seen the way they interact. From what I've seen and heard, it was important for them to keep their word to Camryn to visit Max, and they wanted to support her." Her laugh was wry. "All they wanted was a holiday. Rest, relaxation, and some fruity drinks. Max loves his sister, and I'm trying to be supportive. I don't want to do anything to hurt my husband. I admit it's taking work accepting reality, but I'm trying, and they won't be here for much longer."

Max went to his wife and wrapped his arm around her shoulders. He gave her a quick, affectionate kiss. "Thank you."

"She's your sister, Max. It was hard having her around at first, and I was scared stiff she'd hurt you or Luke. But she enabled us to have our first holiday in years. I know you wouldn't have been happy leaving the horses with the employees. Having her around allowed the rest of the employees to have a holiday too."

"I don't know what to do," Marcus said. "At first I thought I should just let Amme leave, but the idea of letting her go makes my chest hurt."

"Amme seems lovely," Max said. "Would it be so bad having her around? You love her, right?"

"Yes." No problem admitting that. "But what about you, Ellen? She'd need your support."

Ellen hesitated, glanced at her husband then nodded. "You'll have to be patient with me. I'll do my best. Amme saved Autumn from that woman at great personal cost. That means a lot to me," Ellen said.

"What if she gets hurt again?" Marcus had trouble forcing the words past the lump in his throat, and they emerged hoarse and tight with anxiety. "I can't take her to see a doctor or to a hospital. And her friends wouldn't be here to fix her."

"Marcus," Ellen said in a sharp voice. "Can you hear yourself? That's like saying you're never leaving the house again because you might get hurt or...or forcing Autumn not to play with other children because someone might injure her. Accidents happen, and none of us should stop living because of silly fears."

Marcus frowned. Put that way, his worries seemed trivial.

"Are you still having the party tonight?" Ellen asked.

Marcus nodded. "You and Max are bringing Luke? And coming for dinner?"

"Yes," Ellen said. "I want to make my peace with Camryn before she leaves. Max said it might be a while before she's able to make a return visit. Something about visiting Ry's planet of birth?" She shot a glance at Max, and he smiled, understanding and proud. He squeezed her lightly. "I was holding a grudge against Camryn, and I need to apologize to her. I've never seen Max happier, and that makes me happy, too."

Marcus nodded thoughtfully. Each time he considered letting Amme go, something frayed inside him. She'd brought color to his life, and he didn't want to return to the way he'd been living. All business and seriousness with random women thrown in to relieve the boredom. He had a child to consider, his sister...

"She wouldn't have official papers, a birth certificate," he said.

"Marcus, you have pots of money. Surely you could find a way to sort that out? It's not as if you're intending to use false papers for crime," Ellen said.

Max barked out a laugh.

"I know a bit of first aid," Ellen continued. "Maybe if we get them to show us how to avert potential problems, we can act as a medical backup."

Max kissed Ellen before speaking again. "Thank you, Ellen. I know this isn't easy for you. I think that's a great idea. So if you love her, Marcus, all you need to do is convince her to take a chance on you."

"It's too late to get a marriage license because of the public holidays, but we could have a commitment ceremony after Camryn and Ry get married," Marcus said, the burden he'd felt weighing him down lifting. The final decision was easy. The solution boiled down to the fact he loved her, and seeing her leave would leave him an empty husk.

"Sorted?" Ellen asked.

Marcus grinned. "Thanks. Wish me luck."

CHAPTER ELEVEN

During the short drive home, Marcus considered various ways to approach Amme. There was no doubt he'd hurt her when he'd pushed her away and told her he needed time. Somehow, he needed to fix this. He could buy flowers, champagne...

No.

Honesty.

He'd tell her everything—his fears, his concerns, his love.

And if that failed, he'd produce his ring and beg because if she left, he thought something in him would break.

He saw Nanu and Kaya as soon as he climbed out of his car. "Do you know where Amme is?"

"Why?" Kaya asked, her attitude hostile.

"I intend to beg her forgiveness," Marcus said.

"She's inside," Nanu said. "Don't hurt her, Marcus."

"I don't want to hurt her."

"You'd better not," Kaya said, and a sliver of fear sped through him. They'd all seemed happy and harmless. He was beginning to understand he'd seen what he wanted to see. All of them, including Camryn, would make bad enemies.

Marcus offered a curt nod and strode inside. "Amme?"

"We're in the kitchen," Olivia called.

Marcus stalked in that direction. "I need to speak with Amme. Alone," he added. "If that's all right with her." Unusual nerves juddered at the pit of his belly. He had to get this right first off because time wasn't exactly a luxury for them, not with everyone leaving on the second.

"Is that all right with you, Amme?" Camryn asked.

Amme met his gaze and frowned. Finally, she nodded. "Could we go for a walk in the garden?"

"She means so that none of us can listen in," Camryn said.

Marcus felt his brows lift. "You can do that?"

"Certainly. Especially me," Camryn said with a grin.

Amme moved past him, graceful and whole again, her long legs tanned beneath the pair of chocolate-brown shorts she wore. Marcus followed her out into the rose garden near the tennis court.

"Are we far enough away here?"

"Should be but I don't mind if Camryn hears," Amme said. "What did you want to talk about?"

"You. Us." He studied her reaction. "Seeing you crumpled at the bottom of the stairs... God, I thought you were dead."

"I'm a cyborg. A simple fall won't kill me."

"I know that now." He reached for her hands and threaded their fingers together. "I love you, Amme. I've never wanted or thought about another woman in the same way I think about you. I've never ever considered marriage or family, but thanks to you, I've changed. You make me laugh. You make me think, and I love experiencing life through your viewpoint." Marcus stopped talking. This was way worse than doing a business presentation. He sucked in a fortifying breath and plunged onward. He pulled the ring he'd chosen from his pocket. "Will you marry me?"

Amme's hand tightened around his.

"I thought I disgusted you," she whispered, focusing on him instead of the ring.

"God, no! No, please, don't ever think that. I was surprised. Shocked. Concerned because all I could think was what might happen if you got hurt again. The next time you mightn't be so lucky. I talked to Ellen and Max, and they reminded me to embrace life. Sweetheart, I'm sorry for the brain fritz, sorry you got hurt, and I made the pain worse with my bloody stupid reaction." He cruised his fingers over her jaw, thumbed her bottom lip, and his chest swelled with the love he couldn't seem to contain. "I love you, Amme. I want to enjoy every moment we can have together instead of worrying about what might happen. I want to spend my life with you. Please marry me."

"But I'm an alien."

"No problem. We'll get you identification papers somehow. Ry managed to apply for a marriage license, so we can do it too. That's the easy part. The hard part will be staying when your friends leave."

"You don't mind that I'm an alien? That I'm different?"

"To me, you're Amme. You're Amme, the woman who makes me laugh, the woman who bowls me over with her beauty and goodness, the woman who I love so much it hurts. I can't imagine life without you, don't want to think about it. So, will you marry me?"

"I can't have children."

His laugh held indulgence, a touch of exasperation. "I don't care. Children have never been on my horizon, not until Autumn. If there comes a time when we decide we'd like more children, maybe we can adopt. Amme, you're the one who's important to me."

"My programming will lead me to search out a child once Autumn is grown. I can't help it. It...it's an instinct."

"Hell." He raked a hand through his hair, mind busily searching for a solution. "What about if you found a job that puts you in contact with children? Maybe you could work at a school or in a kindergarten. You could train in childcare. Or maybe we could foster children. I'm sure we can work out a solution. We have time, right? Since Autumn is still young?"

Amme nodded. A tear leaked from one eye and rolled down her cheek.

Panic burst inside Marcus. Fear. "God, I'm sorry. I didn't mean to make you cry. I get it. Your friends are leaving, and you'd be alone here and always in danger of discovery. It's too much to ask of you." He tugged his hand free and stuffed the ring into his pocket with his other hand. "I won't bother you again."

"No! Don't go." She seized his arm, clutching it to the point of pain. "Ask me one more time."

Marcus stared at her beautiful face, his heart leaping halfway up his throat. His hand bore a distinct tremor when he reached into his pocket and pulled out the ring for a second time. "Marry me, Amme. I love you, and I don't want to be alone. The best life I can envision has you in it."

"Yes," she whispered, and her smile bloomed into a full-out grin—a blaze of happiness and perfect white teeth. "Oh, Marcus. I love you too. The idea of leaving you and Autumn keeps making me leak. Yes, I'd love to marry you and Autumn." And she threw herself at him. The ring went flying, but he didn't care because she was in his arms. She was staying with him. He kissed her, the rightness of the moment bringing serious leakage to his eyes—not that he'd ever admit it to anyone.

"She said yes. She said yes," Camryn shrieked in the distance. "They're getting married!"

"I thought we were out of earshot," Marcus said.

"She is a leopard shifter." Amme laughed up at him, ablaze with happiness. "Her hearing is exceptional. Mine is good, too. You should remember that for the future."

"No secrets, huh? I love you so much, sweetheart. Thank you for agreeing to stay." And he kissed her again before searching for the diamond ring, which lay somewhere at their feet.

Music filled the air, and the party was in full swing, with Tarzan mingling with Little Bo Peep, a walking carrot, and a sprinkling of aliens. Marcus guided Amme through the crowd of friends and neighbors, introducing his fiancée to everyone he knew.

Finally, they neared their friends.

Camryn, dressed in jockey silks, stood beside Ry, who was a suave James Bond. They were chatting with a sheriff and a pregnant saloon girl, otherwise known as Max and Ellen.

"Ellen seems to be warming to Camryn and her friends," Marcus said in an undertone.

Amme nodded. "I'm pleased for Camryn. She says she was in a bad place before Ry snatched her. Ellen has been slow to forgive. Understandable. She's worried about her children. I appreciate her stance. Camryn does too. But I like Ellen. She's been nice to me, and I think we'll become good friends despite the alien thing."

"That's great. Would you like to dance?" Marcus asked. "Don't worry, it won't be anything fancy."

"Yes, please."

The light caught the sparkling stones on her ring, and her sweet smile tightened his chest. Happiness. Now that he had it, he didn't intend to let go.

On the dance floor, he took her in his arms and started shuffling in time with the music.

Amme lay her head on his shoulder. "I love you, Marcus."

He brushed a gentle finger over her chin, emotion swelling inside him until he struggled to contain the surge. He swallowed, pushing aside the memory of nearly losing her. "And I love you. Have your friends enjoyed their visit?"

"Thanks to you. We've had the best time, and they're already talking about a return visit when time permits," Amme said.

"They have an extra good reason to detour now. Your friends are welcome anytime," Marcus said. "I want you to be happy."

"Your friends now too." She brushed a kiss over his mouth. "I'm very happy, Marcus. I have everything I want right here with you."

"It's almost midnight." Marcus stopped dancing to signal the DJ to halt the music. Silence fell and everyone peered at him in expectation.

"Thanks for coming to share the beginning of the New Year with me and my beautiful fiancée." He checked his watch then slipped his arm around her waist. "Does everyone have their whistles or their favorite person handy? Time for the countdown to begin. Ten. Nine..."

Amme leaned into him. "Eight. Seven..."

"...Six, five, four, three, two, one." Everyone chanted the countdown together.

"Happy New Year," Marcus shouted, and the cry echoed through the large room and spilled out onto the terrace and into the garden. Whistles shrieked and popping sounds indicated the spill of colorful streamers. The partygoers exchanged kisses and exuberant embraces.

"Happy New Year," Amme said, beaming. She stepped into his arms, and he kissed her, happiness huge and overwhelming inside him. He was the luckiest man alive, and he knew it.

The wedding, New Year's Day

A small group stood in the garden with the celebrant.

"I'm nervous," Camryn said as she peered out the window at her friends and family.

Amme patted her hand. "You love Ry. You're already mates. This is the fun bit you get to do because of your mixed races. You should enjoy the moment. Besides, you need to show off your beautiful dress."

Camryn glanced down at her dress—a plain white gown molded her upper torso before flaring out in a full skirt. Embroidered flowers and beads on the bodice took the dress from simple to special. Camryn's dark hair piled up high while her eyes appeared bigger due to the judicious use of makeup. Camryn's peach-colored toenails peeked from her white wedges and matched the posy of apricot roses she clutched in her hands.

"You're right. I'm ready." She lifted her chin and strode into the room where Max waited for her.

"Wait," Amme said, hand darting out to grab her friend's arm. "You've been spending too much time with Jannike and Kaya. Walk slower, with dignity. This is a wedding, not a war."

"I want to get to Ry," Camryn said.

"She's right," Max said. "Make him wait a little. You look beautiful, sis. Mum and Dad would be proud. Gabriel, too," he added, offering his arm.

"You think?" Camryn asked.

"I think Gabriel would like Ry," Max said. "I bet he's cheering from heaven."

Camryn closed her eyes for a brief sec, then opened them and gave a brilliant smile. "I think so too, but I hope he doesn't peek in on our wedding night."

Max barked out a laugh. "Thanks for putting that vision in my mind."

Amme chuckled because she understood Camryn's eagerness and her touch of trepidation. She felt the same way about Marcus.

At a more decorous pace, Max guided Camryn outside into the garden. A saxophonist started playing the wedding march as they passed the first bed of roses.

A male celebrant—rotund and serious in a black suit—stood with Ry under an arbor twined with flowers and ribbons. Potted roses surrounded the arbor in a semicircle, and the sweet scent of the flowers filled the air.

Amme waved at Autumn and Marcus and flashed a grin at her friends and Olivia. Ellen stood with Luke. She waved at Max and Camryn and blew her husband a kiss. The Indy crew clapped, and Ellen, Olivia, and Marcus joined in with the applause. A crack appeared in the celebrant's grave demeanor, and his lips twitched.

The music halted when Camryn reached Ry's side, and the celebrant began the ceremony.

Amme listened to the heartfelt exchange of vows, and contentment settled over her like her favorite butter-soft yakish coat.

"I now pronounce you man and wife," the celebrant said.

Ry wrapped his arms around Camryn and kissed her long and tenderly.

Everyone cheered, and cameras snapped.

When calm returned, the celebrant said, "Now, I have one more special ceremony to complete. Marcus and Amme."

"Amme," Marcus smiled at her, and she took his arm, even though she didn't understand what was happening. "We can't get married yet, because we don't have a license, but I want to commit myself to you in front of your friends. The celebrant agreed to perform the ceremony for us."

Camryn and Ry stepped aside to join the rest of their friends.

"Go on," Camryn said, giving Amme a shunt in the small of her back. "We're taking photos and everything."

Amme stepped over to Marcus and accepted his hand.

"Is it time now, Daddy?" Autumn piped up.

"Soon, sweetheart. You can come and stand by me so you're ready," Marcus said.

"You can say your vows now," the celebrant said.

Marcus dipped his head in a slight nod and shifted to look at Amme. "You have become my best friend in a short time. Having you at my side has filled a gap I didn't realize I had in my life. My love for you is bigger than the Earth, bigger than the universe, and I can't believe how lucky I am that you return my sentiments. I intend to love and cherish you and can't wait to start our life together. Thank you for agreeing to be my wife." He squeezed Amme's hands then glanced down at his daughter. "Your turn, squirt."

"I'm not a squirt," Autumn informed him.

A ripple of laughter came from behind them, and Marcus's lips quivered.

"I'll remember that," he said. "You can talk now. Can you remember what to say?"

"Yes. I promise to be good and pick up my toys when you tell me. Daddy said I should promise to eat Brussel sprouts, but I don't know what they are. Mostly, I'm gonna be good. Is that all right?"

Marcus's grin widened when he noticed Amme's misty smile and the roll of a tear down her cheek. He reached over and smoothed it away. "Perfect, Autumn. Well done!"

"Amme, would you like to say something before I pronounce you officially engaged?" the celebrant asked.

Everyone turned to Amme in quiet expectation. Her mind raced, and a tremor sped to her knees. Thankful she had practiced her English since her arrival and soaked up the language, she began, "I-I l-love you, Marcus, and I love your daughter. I love Autumn as if she were my own child." Her nerves settled, and her thoughts cleared to perfect clarity. "I'm grateful for your acceptance and the way you've welcomed me and my friends into your life. While I'll miss my friends when they leave, I'm excited to start this new journey with you at my side. I wake up each morning with such happy anticipation, and my life is full of joy. I can't wait to be your wife, Marcus. And, Autumn, I can't wait to be part of your family. I promise to be the best wife and mother I can be." She squeezed Marcus's hand then stooped to kiss Autumn on the cheek.

"Are we married now?" Autumn asked.

"Soon," Marcus said, his face aglow with anticipation.

"I now pronounce you officially engaged," the man said.

"Good," Marcus said and promptly kissed her.

She kissed him in return, her mind full of love and the sound of cheers and ribald laughter when the kiss took such a long time. Finally, they parted and turned to their audience.

Marcus lifted their joined hands into the air. "Time to party."

He stayed to talk to the celebrant while everyone else trooped into the house. The house phone started ringing almost as soon as they walked inside.

"I'll get it," Olivia called.

"Time for champagne," Max called. "Sparkling water for you, my dear," he said to his wife.

"Daddy said we have special drinks for us," Autumn said.

"That's right," Max said. "W. A. T. E. R. with bubbles and fruit garnishes."

Marcus walked into the large conservatory where they'd decided to hold Ry and Camryn's wedding breakfast. "The celebrant couldn't stay. He has another wedding in an hour."

Gweneth and Mogens appeared carrying trays of drinks.

"A toast," Max said when everyone had a drink.

"Wait, where's Olivia?" Amme asked. "Is she still on the phone? I'll go and get her." She hurried into the kitchen and found Olivia hunched over with tears streaming down her cheeks.

"Liv, what is it? What's wrong?"

Olivia swiped the tears away and only succeeded in smearing her makeup. "That was my mother. They heard from my friend's mother about my terrible behavior. Since they can't trust me to behave, they've arranged a job for me as a nanny with one of their friends. My mother said if I didn't turn up in Switzerland dressed in a conservative manner with normal-colored hair, they'd disown me. I tried to tell them I didn't want that, but she wouldn't listen. What am I going to do?"

Amme gave Olivia a swift hug then pulled away. "You're going to fix your face and come out to join us in our celebration. Then, once everyone leaves, we'll have a family conference and decide how to handle your parents. I thought you were staying with us? Both Marcus and I would like to have you here."

"Oh, Amme. You're the coolest sister-in-law a girl could have. Marcus is so lucky to have you."

"He is," Gweneth said, appearing from behind them. "We're all going to miss Amme when we leave. Let me help you with your makeup. You don't want to scare Ellen into having her babies too early."

Olivia gave a watery chuckle. "I'm gonna miss you guys as much as Amme."

"We'll be back," Gweneth said in a gruff voice designed to imitate a male star from a movie she'd recently watched.

"I'll leave you two alone," Amme said. "Two minutes, okay? Otherwise, you'll have Marcus out here. We'll work this out, Olivia. I promise."

"That was so much fun," Amme said as she climbed into bed

beside Marcus.

Marcus wrapped his arms around her and drew her against his chest. "I'm going to miss your friends."

"Me too. At least Olivia seemed more cheerful. Your mother upset her. You're not going to let her go to Switzerland, are you?"

"No, not if she wants to stay with us. She said she wants to get a job, but I'm happy to support her until she's financially secure. She asked if we could talk tomorrow."

"Good. That's good."

Marcus rolled them so he was looking down at her startled face. "We'll sort out Olivia tomorrow. Tonight is for us."

Amme grinned up at her fiancé. "I don't have any argument."

Their kiss was unhurried and thorough—a meeting of souls as well as lips. Hands caressed and bodies rocked together, propelling them both into a sea of need. A long time later, Marcus slipped inside her, joining them in the most elemental way.

"I love you," she whispered.

He paused his luscious strokes into her warm depths to smile at her with love and longing. "You have made me the happiest man alive, Amme. I know how much you're giving up to stay here with me, and I intend to spend my days making you happy in return."

Their lips met, the slow plunge into her body and retreat commencing again. Her climax began like the twirl of a ribbon, unfurling and reaching, reaching to frisk her pleasure receptors. She gasped and tumbled into freefall, glorying in this man, her happiness and her renewed sense of purpose.

"Marcus," she gasped, holding tight to his shoulders.

His big frame shuddered, and he stilled, gulping for breath. He kissed her then pressed his forehead to hers. "Thank you for everything."

She felt the hard pull of her lips and the formation of something Camryn said was a dimple. An anomaly for sure, but according to Marcus, cute. "My pleasure, Marcus. I live to make you happy."

"And I live for your happiness, sweetheart."

Amme kissed him, relaxed and happy and fulfilled. A cyborg and a human. A strange mix, to be sure, but it felt right, and that was all that mattered.

Their bodies parted and realigned for comfort, and Amme let her system go into rest, her last thoughts of Marcus and Autumn and happiness.

A childcare cyborg didn't get any luckier.

CHAPTER TWELVE

"Where's Olivia?" Marcus demanded for the fifth time, glancing around myriad bags and milling friends. "She'll miss the takeoff."

"I don't know." Amme frowned as she tried to remember. Now that she thought about it, she hadn't seen Olivia since their shared early morning cup of coffee. In the madness of helping Gweneth and the others pack the last of their Earth souvenirs, she hadn't noticed Olivia.

"Has anyone seen Olivia?" Amme asked.

"Not since earlier," Jannike said. "I'm sorry, but we can't wait any longer. Ry wants us to leave on schedule."

Marcus sighed. "Okay. We'll go. Autumn, are you ready?"

"Yes, Daddy." The little girl jumped into the rear of Marcus's vehicle and waited for Amme to strap her into her car seat. The others piled into the black hire van.

Seconds later, they were following the van and on their way to Max's training stables. Marcus pulled up by Max's SUV, and everyone jumped out.

"I want to come with you," Autumn said.

Amme crouched beside the little girl. "Not today. Just grownups today. You're going to play with Luke. I think Luke's mother said you're going to make ANZAC biscuits—the cookies the mothers made for their soldier sons a long time ago—and bacon and egg pie."

Autumn's brow furrowed, then cleared. She gave a quick nod and trotted over to where Ellen waited with Luke.

One by one, Amme's friends strode over to Ellen and said their goodbyes. One by one, they shook Luke's small hand and patted Autumn on the head.

Camryn joined Amme. "I'm going to miss you. I'm so glad you're happy with Marcus. He's a good man, but part of me still wishes you were coming with us."

Amme turned to her friend. "We'll see each other again."

"Not for hundreds of rotations." Camryn brightened. "But we will return. Ry promised, and he keeps his promises. I can't wait to hear about the changes that will occur in your life. Besides, we can contact you before we leave the solar system in about three days. Why don't I call you each day?" Camryn shot a glance at Marcus, saw he was chatting to Max and Ry. "Have you changed your mind?"

"No." Amme's reply was instant, and some of the angst dancing in the pit of her gut dispersed at the realization. She would miss her friends, but she did want to stay with Marcus. "I love Marcus."

Camryn squeezed her hand. "He loves you too. Don't worry. You have Max and Ellen for backup."

"I do. Don't worry about me. You're the one who's flying into the unknown."

"No guts, no glory," Camryn muttered, and they both laughed.

"Time to go," Ry said.

Like the rest of the crew, Amme picked up a couple of bags and followed Ry as he trekked through the paddocks toward the spot where the Indy waited for their departure.

"Holy Hannah," Amme said after a while. "Who belongs to this bag?"

"Um, that's mine," Kaya said, her bright blue hair flashing in the sunlight. None of them had bothered with disguises this morning since they were leaving.

"It feels as if you have bricks in here," Amme said.

"No, white chocolate," Kaya said. "I wanted enough to last for most of the voyage. It's like the food of gods."

"You couldn't have taken it to the ship yesterday?" Amme asked and resettled the bag over her other shoulder.

"She did," Jannike said. "During the small hours of this morning, she dragged me down to the twenty-four hour supermarket to purchase more."

"You won't be so smartass when I share my bounty," Kaya said.

Fifteen minutes later, they arrived at the Indy.

"Great camouflage," Marcus said. "I could walk past and not notice a thing."

"Job done," Nanu said and nudged Camryn. "Told ya we wouldn't have any trouble."

"We haven't left yet," Camryn said. "Someone could still knock us out of the sky."

Nanu's braids clicked when he shifted position. "The shields are fully active. Not one of Earth's security forces will see us on their instruments. I'm damn good at my job."

Camryn gave one of his braids a sharp tug. "Big-headed too."

"I wish Olivia was here to see. It's probably not safe to take a photo," Marcus said.

"No, not of the Indy." Ry opened the door and stood aside. "Stow the luggage, and then we're off."

Amme caught Mogens peering at the clouds on the horizon. A swirl of black swept across his face like a network of veins.

"What's wrong?" she demanded.

"I don't like the look of the clouds. We should go now."

Ry exchanged a glance with Camryn. "Move it."

Camryn clasped her twin in a tight hug. "Look after Amme for us."

"Will do," he said. "Come back soon."

Camryn bit her lip, nodded briefly, and sought her husband's arms.

"Bye!" Amme said. "Stay safe." She turned and tromped off the Indy.

Marcus joined her and slipped his arm around her waist. Max trotted from the ship and came to a standstill beside them.

"Are we far enough away here?" he asked.

"No, we should stand by the trees," Amme said. "With the shields on, we won't see much."

Once in position under the trees, they turned to watch the ramp pull up and blink from sight. A roar had Amme clapping her hands over her ears, and Marcus and Max followed suit.

Wind snatched their clothing and hair, but gradually, the noise and commotion retreated.

"Whoa," Max said. "Look at the crater and the toppled trees."

"We had a bad landing," Amme said.

Marcus's brows rose as he stared at the carnage. "A bad landing? It's a wonder you walked off the ship."

"Jannike struck her skull. She suffered the sole injury," Amme said. "She bounced back quickly enough."

"Hell," Marcus muttered. "Just how dangerous is it flying through space?"

Amme shrugged. "No worse than crossing a street in the middle of Auckland. Besides, Jannike, Kaya and Ry are highly trained. Camryn is a shapeshifter. She's as dangerous as the other crew members."

"Camryn, dangerous?" Max laughed, then sobered when Amme didn't return the sentiment.

"I saw her when Amme was hurt. Her and Ry," Marcus said. "I'm with Amme. Your twin can hold her own."

"What about you, Amme?" Max asked with a sidelong glance.

"If someone attacks Autumn or Luke or any other child in my care, I'd turn into a dangerous weapon."

Marcus's brows rose. "I don't know whether to believe you or not, but you did save Autumn."

"Believe," Amme said, then spoiled her announcement by laughing.

"Huh," Marcus said and checked his watch. "Might as well wander back. I still thought Olivia would turn up. Mum must have upset her worse than she let on to me. Have you tried the house, Amme?"

"Not since we arrived at Max's farm."

"You worried about her?" Max asked.

"Trouble with the parents." Marcus heaved a heavy sigh. "She's an adult. Guess I need to remember that too."

"But you're not trying to bully her," Amme said. "Your mother and father are treating her like a child."

"Families," Max said. "There's no one better at pushing buttons than family."

"True," Marcus said. "I guess she'll turn up when she's ready."

"Are you guys coming in for a cup of tea?" Max asked.

"Yes, please," Amme said. "I want to see the ANZAC biscuits. Ellen said she'd show me how to make them and lend us a book so I can read the story about the history of the cookies and their place in the history of my new country. It sounds like something I need to know."

Amme spent two hours with Ellen and the children while Marcus went out with Max to help with farm chores.

"Any luck with Olivia?" she asked Marcus when he returned, and they were driving home.

"No, but she still has a few friends in the Auckland area. She's probably gone to visit one of them. I know she hates goodbyes. Always has since she was a kid, so that might have been the reason she left."

"The house seems so quiet. It's going to take a while to get used to not having everyone around."

"What are you doing for the rest of the day?" Marcus asked.

"I don't know. Some housework. Maybe I'll clean out the cottage, although Gweneth promised me she'd checked everything was clean."

"Plenty of time to do that tomorrow or later in the week. Why don't you and Autumn come and help me shift the alpacas to a new paddock?"

"Yes." Amme clapped her hands together. "I like that idea."

Marcus kept her and Autumn busy for the entire afternoon.

Later that night, when Autumn was in bed and she and Marcus were watching a movie, Amme's ear com had her straightening from Marcus's arms. "Camryn?"

"It's me," her friend said. "No problems this end. We've made good time since we found a flight gate. Ry says we'll exit the solar system tomorrow."

Marcus wrapped his arm around her shoulders and drew her close.

"So just one more call," Amme said.

"Yes. Nanu said he can wire our coms so we can all say goodbye. We'll call around the same time tomorrow."

"I'll ask Max and Ellen over for dinner," Amme said. "You'll want to say goodbye to them too."

"Thanks." Tears wobbled within Camryn's speech. She coughed and changed the subject. "We were looking at our photos on our tablets. Nanu has worked out a way for us to charge them. I think we'll be talking about this holiday for years. Oh, Kaya wants to know if Olivia turned up."

"She's staying with a friend for a few days. There was a message on the answer phone when we returned from shifting the alpacas. Marcus said she's never liked goodbyes and probably freaked at the idea of so many at once."

"Glad to hear it," Camryn said. "Kaya locked up her chocolate and threatened Nanu with her blaster when he tried to steal a bar. Mogens is hoarding sweets, too. He had some hidden in his medicine satchel. I know chocolate when I smell it."

Amme chuckled, imagining the scene. "I'm going to ask your brother to teach me to ride. Autumn too, if she wants. The one quick lesson we had before Christmas made me want to learn more. What do you think?"

"That's a great idea. What does Marcus think?"

"I don't know. I just thought of it. No, it's all right. He's smiling and nodding. Marcus suggested I attend a school to get a formal childcare qualification. Sort of prepare for when Autumn is grown."

"Another good idea. You know you can try lots of things. New hobbies and interests," Camryn said, her enthusiasm transmitting through the com. "That should be fun. What are you going to do tomorrow?"

"We're going to take down the Christmas tree in the morning, and we're going to visit Rangitoto Island. Marcus said it's a boat ride, and we can walk to the top of the dormant volcano crater. We're taking a picnic."

"Sounds like fun. We're all in fitness training and practicing with weapons. Ry wants us prepared for anything when we arrive on Viros. Oh, and we're definitely stopping to visit Kaya's brother. Ry is muttering something about adding more guns so we might be there a few days. We're going to lose contact. Nanu said we're going to pass through some meteor fragments. I'll call you tomorrow before we're out of range."

"Okay. Give our love to everyone," Amme said and clicked off. "They've made better time than expected and will be out of range after tomorrow."

"We'll all miss them. If Max doesn't have time to teach you to ride, we'll take lessons. Me too. How does that sound?"

"Yes. I wondered if we could get a puppy-creature. I think it would be good for all of us. Camryn said there are places where you can adopt unwanted creatures."

"A puppy." He nodded in approval. "Let me get my laptop, and we'll see what's available for adoption."

"We're getting a puppy-creature. I mean puppy," Amme said the next night before Camryn could speak. "Max and Ellen rang to say they couldn't come. Ellen isn't feeling well, and Max wanted her to rest. They said to say goodbye."

"It's Ry."

"What's wrong?" Amme said immediately.

"I need to speak with Marcus," Ry said. "It's important."

"He's in his office. I'll go and get him."

"He should be able to hear me through your com if you put your heads close together. Nanu assures me that should work."

Worried now, Amme ran to find Marcus. "It's Ry. He needs to speak to you." She plonked on his knee before he could speak. "If we sit close, you'll be able to hear."

Marcus took her hand in his and squeezed gently. "We're both here, Ry."

"I take it you haven't heard from Olivia?"

"No, but I didn't expect to since she said she was spending a few days with her friend," Marcus said.

"She's here on the *Indy*," Ry said.

"Pardon?" Marcus exchanged a glance with her. "What, Ry? I just thought you said she's with you."

"Gweneth helped her get on board the *Indy* and has kept her hidden. I was sure I could scent her, but Gweneth said it was her sweater. She lied," Ry snapped, and there was no mistaking his testy tone. "The thing is, we're too far from Earth to bring her back. I'm sorry. I know it's going to cause problems."

Amme took one glance at a flummoxed Marcus and seized the opportunity to talk. "What do you suggest?"

Camryn interrupted. "We have two options. We can leave Olivia with Kaya's brother on Slyvia. He's a trader, and she'd be safe there, plus she should manage to find work. Kaya's brother has a housekeeper, so she could stay with him. Kaya just said he's hardly ever at home. The other alternative is taking her to Viros. None of us have been there before."

"What does Olivia say? Could she get transport back to Earth if she stayed on Slyvia?" Amme asked.

"Olivia is refusing to talk." Camryn sounded grim and disapproving. "Gweneth isn't talking either, and they're both in disgrace."

"What do you think is best?" Marcus asked.

"If it were me, I think she'd do better on Slyvia," Camryn said. "The planet is advanced and peaceful. If Olivia uses her brain, she'll find opportunities, and it's helpful that Kaya's brother is there. I trust him. Ry trusts him, too."

"Amme, what do you think?" Marcus asked.

Amme didn't hesitate. "Slyvia would work best."

"Slyvia, it is," Ry said. "We're almost at the next gate. I'll hand you over to Camryn."

"Thank you, Ry," Marcus said. "I'm sorry about Olivia. I had no idea."

"Neither did I." Ry's voice held grimness, and Amme felt a little sorry for Olivia and Gweneth. "It won't happen again. Wait, here's Olivia. I'll put her on."

"Marcus?"

"I'm here."

"Are you angry with me?"

"Not really. I just wish you'd talked to me, to Camryn and Ry first, rather than putting them in this position."

"I know. I'm sorry I've caused trouble, but I'm not sorry I'm in the middle of space. Marcus, it's incredible. Earth from space. Wow."

Amme imagined Olivia shaking her head, her incredulous expression and smiled because she understood the wonder of new and shiny, the buzz-buzz-buzz of excitement. "Camryn and Ry are suggesting that you stay with Kaya's brother. Are you okay with that?"

"I guess. I should talk to Ry," Olivia said.

"Definitely," Marcus said. "Ask for advice before jumping feet first into a new situation, especially up there. Okay?"

"Will do," Olivia said, sounding more cheerful.

"Make yourself useful, meantime."

"Don't think I'll have a choice. Ry is muttering about punishments and cleaning something," Olivia said. "Camryn wants to talk to Amme. Bye. I love you guys."

Amme chatted to Camryn for a few mins, told her about the puppy they hoped to adopt, and started to say her final goodbyes. Halfway through, the com cut out. After secs of static, Amme clicked off and removed the earpiece.

"Are you okay? What are you going to tell your parents about Olivia?"

Marcus snorted out a laugh. "Not the truth, that's for sure. Maybe we can tell them she's gone traveling and is backpacking through South America. If I'm lucky, they won't contact me for a week or so and give me time to work out a strategy."

"Tell them she's staying with a friend while she decides what she wants to do with her future," Amme said. "That's the truth, after all."

"I think I'll finish this later," Marcus said. "There's nothing urgent in the email that can't wait. Why don't we have an early night?"

Amme frowned. "I am not tired, Marcus. I don't wish to sleep."

Marcus's grin turned wolfish. "Sleeping wasn't what I had in mind."

"Ah," said Amme, and she took his hand, ready to walk into the future at his side.

The adventure continues with *Stranded & Seduced* and *Seized & Seduced*. Please turn the page to read an excerpt.

Happy reading,
Shelley xx

EXCERPT – STRANDED & SEDUCED

The bastard had left!

Cimmaron Zhaan stared around the empty transport bay, shock kicking her in the gut. She strode a tight circle to survey her surroundings—just to make sure. Her footsteps resounded in the cavernous spaceport. A droid scooted in front of her, and she snarled under her breath, sidestepping to dodge the worker. Empty. The echo of her boots mocked her, underlining her stupidity in trusting anything the captain said. The *phrullin'* male had taken off early, leaving her stranded with minimal possessions and even fewer credits to her name.

Stranded.

Anger burned through her, and her hands fisted then squeezed as she imagined wringing the captain's beefy neck. The weight of stares from the maintenance crew jerked her from pissed to controlled and inscrutable. Yeah, she'd known the arrogant bastard had expected her to act grateful when he'd suggested they while away the long voyage from Risches to Stavek by sharing a cabin. She'd turned him down flat, and he'd transferred his attentions to one of the lesser crew. But Campbell hadn't forgotten her slight. In fact, he'd gone out of his way to make her life difficult. Leaving her stranded on isolated Marchant was the latest in a long line of Campbell-created annoyances.

Cimmaron stalked past the maintenance men and their droid workers with her nose in the air. Inside, she seethed. What the hell was she gonna do now? Campbell had told her to wear mufti while on leave, so she didn't even have a uniform to prove she was a pilot. All her papers were on the *Intrepid*. She stormed down a long corridor to the communication center, this method of contact the best way to ensure he accepted her call. One hour later, the telecommunications tech put her through to command on the *Intrepid*.

"Ah, Officer Zhaan." Campbell sat at ease in the pilot's chair, his tunic blindingly white while his dark eyes bore a trace of smugness.

Bastard. "Captain Campbell." Cimmaron jammed the tip of her tongue behind her teeth instead of blurting the obscenities she wanted to level at him.

"You were late. We had our allocated time slot to depart."

Cimmaron's eyes narrowed, but she refused to react any further, giving him the leverage to land her in even deeper crap.

"This will go on your record, Officer Zhaan."

Too late. It seemed the situation was already beyond mere apologies and groveling. "You told me we were leaving at second moonrise."

"First moonrise," he countered. "Officer Zhaan, I have noted on your record you are AWOL."

"You lied. You told me second moonrise."

The tinge of red on his prominent brow warned her she should've held her tongue. His pointy ears twitched—a sure sign

201

of impending displeasure. "None of the other crew was late back from leave."

Cimmaron's nails dug into her thighs, and the heat of temper crawled across her cheekbones. *Phrull*, she was probably flashing gold with her emotions, sparkling like the backside of a glow bug—an unfortunate side effect of being a Dlog. "Are you going to come back for me?"

"Return for one female. I don't think so. Officer Zhaan, I'd say you're officially screwed." A smirk formed on his lips, echoing in his sly eyes. "Over and out."

The *phrullin'* bastard. The need to scream swelled inside her. She wanted to punch and kick and exert bodily harm on the slimy male. He might have screwed her chances of flying with the Coalition again, but she'd exact her revenge. One day, when he was least expecting her move. She exited the communications room with precise steps, her back stiff with pride. The five staff manning communications had heard everything. It was obvious by the silence that even now spilled out of the room after her, taunting and full of ridicule.

Desperate to outrun her fears, the panic threatening to overwhelm her, Cimmaron stormed from the spaceport and pushed into the crowd thronging the narrow alleys outside.

Market day. Locals shopped and hustled. Visitors purchased supplies to fill dwindling reserves on their short stopovers between destinations. Traders and hawkers shouted at the tops of their voices, trying to attract customers and extract credits. No doubt thieves trolled the alleyways, looking for the green and unwary who carried purses full of gold for the taking. She had no idea where she was going or what to do.

Blindly, she attempted to control her blooming panic, the knowledge that the captain's petty revenge had left her vulnerable and in big trouble. Her record would reflect the transgression unless she could prove her innocence. She'd have to travel to

Coalition headquarters on Bezant. Somehow. It wasn't going to be easy with no currency to pay for her passage. The rumors of space pirates and abductions in this galaxy meant people were wary of giving strangers rides.

Deep in thought, she bumped into a short, blue female, almost knocking her to the ground.

"Sorry," Cimmaron said.

"Hoy, watch it." The female struggled to maintain her footing on the slick cobblestones.

Cimmaron grabbed the female's upper arm, holding her upright when the crush of humanity behind threatened to push her to the cobblestones. "My apologies," she said in a formal tone when the danger was past.

The female righted the white cowl covering her shiny, pale blue head and glanced at the splotches of mud decorating the hem of her robe. "I look like a low-caste." A trace of alarm flickered over her face. "*Phrull*, I need this job."

"Job?"

"They're hiring at the club. I must go. They'll close the doors when they have enough applicants." The female darted through a gap in the crowd before Cimmaron could question her further.

The female's words kept reverberating through her mind. A job. A job. *A job.*

A rumbling sound punctuated her thoughts, and she bolted after the female, elbowing her way through the alley crowded with market goers as she tried to follow. No currency. She would starve, and she had to eat. A job was the solution—the only alternative she had if she wanted to leave this goddess-forsaken planet and exact revenge from that *phrullin'* bastard Campbell.

Visit my website to learn more
(https://shelleymunro.com/books/stranded-seduced/)

EXCERPT – SEIZED & SEDUCED

A shrill cry echoed through the arid valley. Unexpected, it set a shudder rippling the length of her body. Jannike Hondros, second-in-command of the *Indefatigable*, came to an abrupt halt, her stomach twisting anxiously even as she grabbed her blaster out of her hip holster and flicked off the safety.

"Tracker lizards." At her side, Ry Coppersmith, captain of the spaceship, confirmed her fears. He edged his petite mate behind him, but despite her size, Camryn O'Sullivan was no pushover.

She neatly sidestepped him, wincing at a repeat head-splitting shriek closer this time. "What are tracker lizards, and why are they making that infernal noise?"

"Trackers are the best available means of tracking an object or person. They never fail to capture their target. *Never.* The cries mean they're on a scent," Jannike said tersely, eyes scanning the far end of the valley. She'd experienced their tenacity before and hadn't emerged on the winning side.

"Us." Ry glanced at Jannike, and with the ease of a long friendship, they came to a decision without words.

Jannike gave him an imperceptible nod. "We need to split up," she said abruptly, attention on the horizon. In the distance, maybe four or five clicks, she caught the swirl of approaching dust. "You need to shift, change your scents."

"But Mogens said shifting might be dangerous." Camryn cupped her slim belly in protest.

"We're going to have to risk it," Ry said without hesitation. "It's either that or capture."

"Capture? What's going on? This sort of thing doesn't happen on Earth. Usually," Camryn added, obviously thinking about her own kidnapping several cycles earlier.

"I'll keep going away from the ship," Jannike said, a lump the size of a rock closing up her throat, making the words gravely. She swallowed dryly, silently cursing both the situation and this god-awful heat from the planet's sun. The dry temperatures sucked the juice from everything, animal and vegetable. "Go." It was surprisingly difficult to force out the order.

Camryn still frowned, not understanding. She squinted at her husband, shifted her attention to Jannike. "But—"

"Change. Now," Ry barked. "Jannike, if you're captured, we'll come for you. We will not give up. That's a pledge."

"Same goes." Secs later, she started running, veering around the pile of rocks and sprinting down the rolling sand hill, away from Ry and Camryn. It had to be the cargo ship they'd seen earlier, but why had they set tracker lizards on them?

A thought sprang into her mind, and she stumbled before regaining her balance. *Holy fukk.* No, it couldn't be *her*. No, that was impossible when Jannike was light years away from her home planet.

Behind her, the baying shrieks of the lizards intensified. Sweat trickled down her forehead, stinging her eyes. She slipped in the shifting sand, arms flailing before she toppled, hitting the ground hard enough to knock the breath from her lungs.

No time to baby herself. She had to move. Faster. She had to give Ry and Camryn time to get to the ship otherwise the entire crew could get sucked into whatever trouble they'd blundered into this day. Her blue tunic clung like a lover. A skin wet from sweat. The dry rocks in her throat closed her windpipe. She panted, a painful wheeze. Gods, she had to keep going. She twisted, rolling and pushing to her feet. She lurched her first steps, only her fitness and determination propelling her forward.

Concentrate on running. Forget the trackers. Don't think about the past.

The landscape stretched endlessly in front of her—one big, inhospitable sandpit. Overhead, the planet's sun beat down, frying everything in its path. And still, she kept trying to run. One foot in front of the other, leading the trackers farther away from the *Indy*. Faster. Faster. The *Indy's* crew were her friends, her family, and she'd do anything to keep them safe.

Determination gave her a burst of speed, but a glance over her shoulder told her the trackers had dramatically closed the distance between them. Their brown-blue bodies glinted in the bright light, strangely beautiful despite their ferocity. Their baying cries filled her head, lent panic to her adrenaline-fueled flight. She rounded a corner and came to an abrupt halt. A box canyon. The wall of rock stretched into the distance as far as she could see.

Trapped.

Nowhere to go.

Slowly, chest rising and falling in uneven gasps, she turned to face the four snapping trackers. Their bulging eyes blinked slowly, their wicked teeth white against the brown-blue of their skin. Their stubby tails shifted lazily from side to side, strong muscles in their haunches poised to spring should she attempt a sudden move.

She edged along the rock wall, and they moved with her. She'd heard their bite was nasty, and some people were highly allergic to their saliva.

But she refused to go without a fight. She reached for a handhold on the rock wall, digging her fingertips, attempted to lever her body upward.

"Ho, my beauties. What have you caught me today?" The mountain of a man rode up on a cyber-beest—a combination of machine and cheetahbeest by the look of the tawny coat and spots. The cyber-beest snorted, pawing at the ground, restive under the firm restraint. The large rider wore a tight, light gray suit shaped to his body. The man was all muscle with no fat. With his left hand, he controlled the cyber-beest while his right rested lightly on a coiled whip.

Jannike glanced left, speared a look right. A tracker bite or the nip of Mountain Man's whip. Both would hurt.

"You won't escape," Mountain Man said with almost a kind smile. But the smile didn't reach his wintry-blue eyes and she knew, deep in her gut, he wouldn't hesitate to do whatever he needed to do to capture her. Fukk, her past had come back to bite her in the bum. There was no other explanation. "Why are you chasing me?"

"Why did you run?" the man countered.

Visit my website to learn more about Seized & Seduced (https://shelleymunro.com/books/seized-seduced/)

ABOUT SHELLEY

USA Today bestselling author Shelley Munro lives in Auckland, the City of Sails, with her husband and a cheeky Jack Russell/mystery breed dog.

Typical New Zealanders, Shelley and her husband left home for their big OE soon after they married (translation of New Zealand speak - big overseas experience). A twelve-month-long adventure lengthened to six years of roaming the world. Enduring memories include being almost sat on by a mountain gorilla in Rwanda, lazing on white sandy beaches in India, whale watching in Alaska, searching for leprechauns in Ireland, and dealing with ghosts in an English pub.

While travel is still a big attraction, these days Shelley is most likely found in front of her computer following another love - that of writing stories of contemporary and paranormal romance and adventure. Other interests include watching rugby (strictly for research purposes), cycling, playing croquet and the ukelele, and curling up with an enjoyable book.

Visit Shelley at her Website
https://shelleymunro.com

Join Shelley's Newsletter
https://shelleymunro.com/newsletter

ALSO BY SHELLEY

Middlemarch Shifters
My Scarlet Woman
My Younger Lover
My Peeping Tom
My Assassin
My Estranged Lover
My Feline Protector
My Determined Suitor
My Cat Burglar
My Stray Cat
My Second Chance
My Plan B
My Cat Nap
My Romantic Tangle
My Blue Lady
My Twin Trouble
My Precious Gift
My Grumpy Wolf

Middlemarch Gathering
My Highland Mate
My Highland Fling
My Elusive Mate
My Valiant Princess
My Highland Wedding
My Highland Billionaire

House of the Cat
Captured & Seduced
Claimed & Seduced
Merry & Seduced
Stranded & Seduced
Seized & Seduced
Hunted & Seduced
Festive & Seduced
Betrayed & Seduced
Enticed & Seduced

Dragon Investigators
Blue Moon Dragon
Blood Moon Dragon
Black Moon Dragon
Snow Moon Dragon

Dragon Isles
Liza
Cherry
Rena
Sasha